"Are you Sue Per...

Janna Whitley stared up at ... before her in the bus depot of the sweltering Arizona town. From where she sat, he appeared to be a long, lean giant.

Or maybe she'd just shrunk. It was entirely possible that since arriving in this state she'd lost not only pounds, but inches from the amount of perspiring she'd been doing.

Janna regarded him uncertainly. This couldn't be Mrs. Carr's partner, could it? A man who was owner of a ranch should be a little more polished and...well, respectable-looking.

She could be wrong, though. Lately she'd been wrong about men more often than she'd been right.

Janna cleared her throat. "No, I'm not Sue, but I'm the woman you're looking for."

Dear Reader,

While writing *The Tenderfoot,* I tried to focus on the kinds of scrapes a city girl could get herself into if she took a job on a ranch. I think we've all been in situations where we don't know quite what we're doing and have to wing it, just as Janna Whitley does in this book. Many of us have also been compelled to help someone out, though we're not sure why, much like the hero, Seth Brody.

In *The Tenderfoot,* Janna has a fascination with cowboys, ranch life and the West that many people share, including me. I feel privileged to be a native Arizonan because I've had frequent contact with the types of interesting characters for which the West is famous—my own father among them. Although he worked in a copper mine, he was from a ranching family and returned to raising cattle after his retirement. He always liked to rope and, when I was young, used to keep in practice by lassoing his three daughters as we ran across the living room! We loved it, but it wasn't very high on my mother's list of ladylike activities.

My father learned most of what he knows about cattle from his sister and brother-in-law, Gladys and Herbert Hynson. Many years ago, they ranched in Arizona's White Mountains where *The Tenderfoot* is set. When anyone mentions "ranchers" to me, they are the ones who come to my mind, and it is to them that this book is lovingly dedicated.

Sincerely,

Patricia Knoll

THE TENDERFOOT
Patricia Knoll

Harlequin Books

TORONTO • NEW YORK • LONDON
AMSTERDAM • PARIS • SYDNEY • HAMBURG
STOCKHOLM • ATHENS • TOKYO • MILAN
MADRID • WARSAW • BUDAPEST • AUCKLAND

ISBN 0-373-03296-X

THE TENDERFOOT

Copyright © 1994 by Patricia Knoll.

This edition published by arrangement with Harlequin Enterprises B. V.

® and TM are trademarks of the publisher. Trademarks indicated with ® are registered in the United States Patent and Trademark Office, the Canadian Trade Marks Office and in other countries.

Printed in U.S.A.

CHAPTER ONE

"ARE YOU SUE PERRITT?"

Janna Whitley stared up at the man who had approached her in the tiny waiting area of the bus depot in the sweltering southeastern Arizona town. From where she sat he appeared to be a long, lean giant—but maybe that was the effect of the narrow-legged jeans, chambray shirt, scuffed boots and black Stetson he wore.

Either that, or she had shrunk. It was entirely possible that since entering this state she had lost inches, not just pounds, from the amount of perspiring she'd been doing.

Janna regarded him uncertainly. Despite the shadow cast by the hat's brim, she could see his face clearly in the noontime sun that was streaming through the wide plate-glass windows. He had a strong chin, a straight, full mouth and dark brown eyes under thick, even brows.

This couldn't be Mrs. Carr's partner, could it? A man who was part owner of a ranch should be a little more polished and . . . well, respectable-looking.

She could be wrong, though. Lately she'd been wrong about men more often than she'd been right.

Whether this was the right person to ask or not, she knew she had to be bold and quick with her request. Her heart quivered, but she stood and held out her hand.

"Are you Mrs. Carr's partner?"

His mouth quirked into a crooked smile. "I'm Seth Brody. Sometimes I'm not sure whether I'm her partner or her gofer. Are you Sue Perritt?"

Janna cleared her throat. "No, I'm not Sue, but I'm the woman you're looking for."

He gave her a skeptical frown but he gripped her hand briefly. His palm was dry and warm—and as tough as a slab of beef jerky. Instantly, she remembered something her businessman father had said. "If a man has calluses, you can cash his check because he's worked hard for whatever he's got."

Seth Brody's hand was also unbelievably strong. Janna drew her fingers away and flexed them surreptitiously as he asked, "How can you be the woman I'm looking for if you're not Sue Perritt?"

This was the moment. She gulped down her panic and gave her most winning smile, "I'm taking Sue's place."

"Says who?"

Janna's smile drooped along with her spirits. She linked and unlinked her fingers, feeling the perspiration on her palms. She had to admit her appearance might not inspire confidence. She knew what he saw: a slim woman of medium height with pale green eyes and curly auburn hair that flew around her head as if each lock was doing business for itself. Her skin was fair, with a hint of freckles across the bridge of her nose. Her chin was marked by the tiniest of clefts. No matter how she tried to make herself seem mature, she appeared young and flighty.

As if that wasn't enough, she was dressed in the type of outfit she would have normally worn at home in Beverly Hills. In fact, she had worn it yesterday, not bothering to change clothes before she fled from there. It was an eye-catching heavy yellow silk slacks and top set made by one of California's trendiest designers.

Unfortunately, it was an ensemble designed for someone who lived in air-conditioned comfort, and was totally unsuited to an Arizona summer day. She was roasting.

Janna had done a great many impulsive things in her life, but what she'd been through in the past twenty-four hours might take the prize for even her headlong acts. But it was too late for regrets. She met his eyes boldly. "Sue has fallen ill and will be hospitalized for—"

"Hospitalized!"

"It's appendicitis. She's at the local hospital—"

"Appendicitis!"

"If you would stop interrupting me, I could explain."

He gave her an irritated look. "You're not doing much of a job of it. I feel like I'm coming in on the tail end of the story here. Why don't you start at the beginning? With your name, for instance."

She opened her mouth and came within a hairbreadth of lying, but she knew that would eventually cause even more problems. Besides, this cowboy had probably never heard of her father: real estate magnate, Ben Whitley. She also doubted he would connect her to her mother, actress Shea Willetta. "I'm Janna Whitley. I met Sue on the bus. We were seatmates." She ended with a slight upswing of tone that had him nodding in understanding. Encouraged, she continued. "She told me she'd once lived in this area and had wanted to move back for a long time and finally found the job with Mrs. Carr."

"And?" His gaze swept over her again, then settled, narrowed and steady on her face. Janna felt as if he was looking straight through her to her jumbled thoughts.

"Then about half an hour before we got here, to, uh—" she had to stop and think of the town's name "—Safford, she doubled over in pain. When we got into town, the driver took her right to the hospital. They diagnosed acute appendicitis, and they're planning to do surgery. She asked me to come and meet you and tell you what had happened. Also, I'm going to take her place working for Mrs. Carr until she's well." She added the last bit with a breathless rush and a shakily hopeful smile.

"I don't think so, Miss Whitman." He turned, his dark eyes sweeping the room, before he stalked toward the bus station door.

Irritated at being dismissed so easily, Janna darted in front of him so he would have to stop and take notice of her. She forced firmness into her voice. "It's Whitley, and I think you should reconsider."

The man took one sliding step around her. "No." He pushed the glass door open and strode into the June afternoon's heat, heading for a pay phone.

Janna's irritation bloomed into fury. Nobody was going to brush *her* off like that! Grabbing her purse and her big suitcase, she marched after him.

No doubt he intended to call Mrs. Carr, tell her about Sue and say that he'd find someone else. He seemed determined not to consider her, but she was equally determined to change his mind. From everything Sue had told her, Janna knew this job would be perfect for her.

As she watched Seth swing through the door she wondered where that Western hospitality she'd read so much about was. Where was the Westerners' belief that people had the right to prove themselves on a job? This cowboy obviously knew nothing about it.

Old Western movies had always fascinated Janna, especially the ones like *My Darling Clementine,* which had been set in Arizona. She'd also read many books on the state, its history and the colorful characters who had founded it. A century before, this territory, a wild combination of desert and mountains, heat and cold, had been settled by people like her who were seeking a new life. That desire was what had lured her to Arizona after she left home.

She barreled through the door behind him, her bags banging against her knees. The desert heat rocked her back onto her heels as if she'd run into a clenched fist. Instantly, sweat popped out on her forehead. She staggered, catching herself against the edge of the hot metal door. She waited for the moment of dizziness to subside before continuing. Her silk outfit didn't let air in, or body heat out, making her feel as though she'd been shrink-wrapped in plastic from head to toe.

Gasping for breath, she teetered after him on rubbery legs.

Everything that had happened to her over the past day had been new to her. Like walking in to the condominium she and her fiancé, Michael, had bought and finding him in bed with his secretary. Listening, shocked, to his taunt that her father had promised him a vice presidency as soon as he and Janna were married. And confronting her father who had confessed that Michael's words were true.

She didn't know who made her more furious—Michael, for being a lecherous jerk, or her father, for trying to manipulate her life. She felt a pang of longing for her mother. If Shea had been home instead of on location in Africa, she would have discovered Ben's machinations and put a stop to them.

Janna swiped at the perspiration that was smudging the last of her makeup. Yes, sir, yesterday had been a real humdinger. So far, today hadn't been much better. She had been too nervous and upset to eat and the sudden illness of the new friend she had made on the bus had scared her. Now she had to convince this hard-headed cowboy to hire her.

By the time she reached Seth Brody's side, he had dialed the phone and was asking the person on the other end about Sue's condition.

As she shamelessly eavesdropped, Janna set her suitcase on end and plopped her roomy shoulder bag on top. Obviously, Seth Brody was a careful man who wanted confirmation of what Janna had told him. She couldn't fault him for that, but if she could help it, she wasn't going to let him make a decision that should be made by Mrs. Carr.

She listened as he spoke briefly to the nurses' station where someone evidently confirmed Janna's story. Before he hung up, he asked the nurse to tell Sue to call Mrs. Emelyn Carr if she needed anything. When he had replaced the receiver on its cradle, he glanced at Janna, who offered what she hoped was a trustworthy smile. "See? I was telling the truth."

"Unfortunately, yes."

When he didn't say anything further, but merely stared at her, she held out her hands again, palms up. "Well, can I have the job until Sue recovers, or not?"

The corners of his mouth crimped downward. "I don't think so."

"Why don't we let Mrs. Carr decide? I'd be working for her, after all."

"I *am* Emelyn Carr's partner, you know, and I don't think you're qualified."

She slapped her hands onto her hips. "How could you possibly know that from looking at me, Mr. Brody? You know nothing about me." She was hot, tired, thirsty, dizzy from the searing sun, more miserable than she'd ever been before in her life, and thoroughly fed up with the entire male gender. "At least give me a chance!"

"I know more about you than you think. I can tell by looking at you that you'd be as out of your element on a working ranch as a heifer at a tea party."

Offended, Janna didn't bother trying to control her expression as she glared at him. "You're wrong!"

He rolled his eyes. "Oh, come on. That outfit you're wearing sure can't be considered work clothes. Your shoes cost more than every pair I own put together, and I'll bet your perfume would set some poor sucker back about two hundred dollars an ounce. I know plenty about you."

"Maybe I'm not like your usual hired hand, but that doesn't mean I can't work." Urgently, she moved closer and shielded her face from the glaring sun so she could look directly into his eyes.

"Have you ever cooked for a dozen hungry men after a day of rounding up and branding cattle?"

She'd never cooked for *any* men, but she wasn't going to tell Seth that and ruin her chances for sure. Still, she wanted to stay as close as possible to the truth. "No, of course not, but I can learn!"

"Ever cooked over a camp fire?"

She gulped. "Camp fire? Well . . ." She almost said no, but she saw an expectant look on his face that changed her mind. She straightened and lifted her chin even higher. It had suddenly developed a tendency to wobble. "I can do it."

Exasperated, he reached up and punched his hat back with his thumb. "Why does it have to be this job, Miss Whitman? There are other jobs you'd be better suited for. Have you tried modeling?"

She would have taken that as a compliment if his tone hadn't held a taunting edge. Her lips drew together as she bit back a sharp reply. How was she going to convince him? She needed this job because it was in a remote area of Arizona where her father and his faithful right-hand man, Alden, would never search for her. It would give her time to think over the catastrophic changes in her life and decide what she wanted to do next. A few weeks of honest work wasn't too much to ask for, was it?

"Because I can do it, Mr. Brody, and—"

"Oh, no," he interrupted, looking over her shoulder.

"Yes, I can," she insisted, warming to her subject. "All I need is a chance...."

"Be quiet for a minute, will you?"

Janna finally realized he wasn't paying attention to her. Confused, she spun around to glance behind her. The quick turn made her head swim, but it settled after a moment. "What is it? What's wrong?"

A small, sporty car, followed by a pickup truck, drove into the bus depot's minuscule parking lot. A woman stepped from the car, and Janna's eyes widened. The newcomer was a pretty blonde wearing a flowered sundress.

Watching her walk toward them, smiling and fresh-looking, Janna felt even hotter and frumpier. Her reaction was mild compared to Seth's, though. It wasn't what she would have expected from a man seeing an attractive woman. His tough face held the pure dread of a husband who'd been asked to hold his wife's purse in public.

"Hello, Mr. Brody," the woman sang out. "Remember me? Melinda Crandall. My mother and I visited Mrs. Carr at the ranch a few weeks ago. I talked to her again this morning, and she said you and your new housekeeper will be happy to help us out with our little project today."

"She would say something like that," Seth muttered. "Sure, I remember you." He gave her a wan smile that told Janna he was about to agree to something he really didn't want to do. "How can I help?"

Janna, feeling sick and light-headed from heat and hunger, gave him a puzzled glance, then forgot about him when her attention focused on the two men who had stepped from the truck. Although they looked no older than her teenage twin brothers, they wore stars pinned to their shirts. Obviously, they were some kind of police officers.

Janna's heart plummeted. Her father had called the police, and they'd found her already. Darn! Now she would never get the chance to be on her own, to prove herself. She had endured the long bus ride and the searing heat for nothing.

Her vision went black for a few seconds, but she shook it off, bracing herself against her suitcase so she wouldn't end up on the asphalt face first. Surely these men weren't going to arrest her. She was of age and had merely left her home, not burned it down. Still, she wasn't going to give Ben Whitley the satisfaction of knowing she had argued and struggled with the officers sent to find her.

Despite their youth, these two looked pretty tough.

Janna experienced another bout of dizziness and steadied herself. As the two men approached, she imagined them to be Arizona Rangers, like those who had brought peace to this part of the country in the last century. Everyone knew they were relentless.

Seth was still in earnest conversation with Melinda Crandall. He hadn't even noticed the two other men. That was probably just as well. Intent on her own thoughts, Janna hadn't heard a word Seth and the woman had said and if she was lucky, she could leave before Seth noticed her being led away like a criminal. Having him see her would have made the humiliation even worse.

Stoically, she lurched forward and gasped, "I guess you're looking for me, Officers. I'm Janna Whitley. I'll come peacefully in spite of what my father may have told you."

Seth broke off his conversation and stared at her, his face full of dismay. "Uh, Janna, no. Don't. We can pay them off...."

"Bribe an officer of the law?" she asked, speaking carefully and taking deep breaths so she wouldn't embarrass herself by throwing up on her Mario Zitti sandals. Shaky, but proud, she said. "My father might do that, but I never would."

The two young men broke into hearty laughter, and one brought a pair of handcuffs out of his pocket. "That's pretty funny, miss! Bribery. We don't know your dad, but I'm glad you're willing to come peace-fully.''

Thoroughly confused now, Janna watched as the man snapped the shiny silver bracelet around her wrist, then reached for Seth's arm. He clicked the cuff into place while Seth gave Janna a glare that was hot enough to brand cattle.

''Why didn't you let me handle it?''

''Well, I . . .''

''Don't worry,'' the perky blond chirped. ''You probably won't be locked up for long.''

''I CAN'T BELIEVE IT! You got us jailed at Wally's Discount City.'' Half an hour later, Seth was still fuming.

Janna knew he would have paced if there had been room—and if he hadn't remained handcuffed to her. As it was, he towered over her, dwarfing the small ''holding cell,'' built of two-by-fours and stacked bales of hay. It had been erected in the space between the checkout counters and the shopping carts.

''Well, how was I supposed to know this was a fund-raising stunt for the junior rodeo? And that Melinda's mother is a friend of Mrs. Carr's and that Mrs. Carr had said you'd help and those guys weren't real cops?'' Janna splayed her uncuffed hand over her chest. ''*I've* never heard of jailing people for charity and having them bail themselves out.''

''You could have listened! Melinda and I were standing right there talking about it. What have you got on your conscience that would make you think your father would send a couple of yahoos wearing tin badges to get you?'' He threw his hands in the air, jerking one of hers up, too. ''Did you think you were in the wild, wild West or something?''

Since she couldn't explain the strange moment when she'd imagined that very thing, without seeming silly, Janna didn't answer. Instead, she looked away and nonchalantly fluffed her hair with her free hand. She was relieved and delighted that the men hadn't been real lawmen. ''It was a simple misunderstanding,'' she said haughtily. ''I don't see why you're so upset about it.''

Seth made a growling sound and his eyes turned black as pitch. ''I'm upset because I don't have my checkbook. Emmie probably wouldn't answer the phone if I tried to call because she's got a crazy idea that I need to get out and socialize more, and this is one way to get me to do it. I was going to mail Melinda a check later, but you spoiled that by volunteering to be jailed. I have hardly any cash, and you already told me that you don't have much money. They won't take credit cards, and—'' he held up their joined hands ''—I'm handcuffed to a woman I hardly know.''

''Well, this isn't a picnic for me, either.''

He ignored her. ''Besides all that, I need to get back to the ranch because I've got a mare about to foal.''

''Well, bully for you.''

He gave her a disgusted look. ''Mares have colts or fillies. Heifers have bulls.''

"Takes one to know one," she muttered under her breath.

She didn't think he'd heard, but she saw Seth control himself with a visible effort. Instead, he said, "You know, if you're really interested in working on my ranch, you'd be better off doing more sucking up and less smart mouthing."

She had the grace to look chagrined. She was being a snot. "Sorry."

He nodded in acceptance. "We've got to get out of this. Any suggestions?"

"Beg, plead and cry?"

He winced. "I'm not going to let you do that while *I'm* around."

"I was suggesting it for *you.*"

"I thought you were going to try and get on my good side."

"You've got one?" When he gave her a direct stare, she realized she wasn't helping her cause. "Sorry, again. Why don't you think of some way to get us out of here?"

"I will." He stood, looking around thoughtfully at the customers streaming by. At a card table a few feet away, a matronly woman sat beside a big sign declaring that the jail-a-thon was for the benefit of junior rodeo riders who wanted to expand their classes to include riding lessons for developmentally delayed children. Volunteers who'd allowed themselves to be jailed could be "bailed out" by donations to the fund. There had been several other people in the cell when Seth and Janna arrived, but they had quickly and cheerfully paid their fines and departed. Only Seth and Janna were left to fume and argue with each other.

"Maybe somebody I know will happen by and bail us out. They're holding this in a busy store for a reason," Seth stated.

"Yeah, to add insult to injury."

"You got us into this."

Janna closed her mouth. The only good thing to be said for the whole situation was that the store was air-conditioned, and the elderly lady in charge had given them fat, juicy hot dogs and big cups of iced soda when they'd been brought in. Janna had devoured hers with a greediness that would have sent her English nanny into a swoon.

One of the bad things about the situation was she was still handcuffed to Seth. Apparently, the two "deputies" had taken the key with them.

The jailer had tut-tutted over that, saying this was the third time it had happened. Unfortunately she had no way of contacting the two young men or Miss Crandall until they came in with more detainees.

Janna and Seth sat side by side on a bale of hay, and she tried not to be aware of the long, sinewy arm and the strong, hair-dusted hand so close to her own. If she was to tell any of her friends at home about this, they would laugh uproariously over it.

She wouldn't laugh, though. She had been so unnerved by the heat and the appearance of the two officers that she had surrendered without thinking. If she had admitted her mistake and refused to participate in the jail-a-thon, she would have looked even more foolish. Besides, she probably would have lost her chance to convince Seth to give her the job *and* seemed like a quitter—the last thing she wanted him to think of her. No, this was not a laughing matter.

There was something about Seth that didn't invite laughter at his expense, even though he had accepted this fiasco in good humor. Well, relatively good humor.

Why was he going along with it? He was certainly forceful enough to have simply told Melinda Crandall he wasn't going to jail for charity, or any other reason, or that he would mail her a check. He'd had no trouble telling Janna no!

He could have told Melinda that Janna wasn't his new housekeeper and that the real housekeeper had been hospitalized. He could have said it would be thoughtless and callous of him to take part in this event when poor Sue was suffering. But that wouldn't have been strictly honest. Sue was in good hands and wouldn't have cared what he did.

It seemed Seth wanted to do what Mrs. Carr expected of him. Janna wondered if that could be his one area of vulnerability and whether she could use it to her own advantage. However, they had to get out of here first. Obviously the only way to do that was to use their assets.

"Well, have you thought of anything?" Seth asked, startling her.

She gave him a nervous smile. "I think so. What about you?"

"Nope. What's your idea?"

"First, I want your word that you'll give me the job."

"My word?"

He seemed flabbergasted, but before he could argue, Janna hurried on. "Oh, please don't turn me down," she begged, laying her free hand on his arm. She felt the muscle jump beneath her palm and hastily drew it away.

Seth was gazing at her with a mixture of wonder and frustration in his dark eyes. "First, you get me jailed. Now you're manipulating me."

That startled her. Surely she wasn't doing to someone else what she resented her father so much for doing to her? Her face flushed as fiery as her hair. "I am not. I'm . . . I'm giving you the opportunity to reconsider," she said firmly.

"Generous of you."

Janna held her breath, waiting. It gave her a heady rush to stand up to him. She knew instinctively that, given time to think it over, he would be fair.

He rubbed his thumb along his jaw for a minute before he answered. "I can't make any promises right now, but we'll talk about this more as soon as we're out of here."

It wasn't as much as she wanted, but it would have to do. She was learning pretty quickly that Seth Brody couldn't be pushed any more than he wanted to be. "All right."

"Now, about your idea?"

"I'm ready, but you'll have to come with me."

Humor glimmered in his dark eyes as he held up their linked wrists. "That much is obvious."

"Well, come on, then."

When she stood and walked to the side of the cell that faced the store's entrance, he pulled her to a stop and gave her a reluctant frown. "What are you going to do? I don't like the look on your face."

She blinked at him innocently. "We've known each other barely an hour. What makes you think this isn't my normal look?"

"Because this one makes me think of sideshow barkers at the county fair."

"You may be close to the truth." She dug in her capacious shoulder bag for a brush, mirror and lipstick. Since she couldn't hold the mirror without his cooperation, she shoved it into his hand. "Here, hold this for me." The small shiny square looked utterly ridiculous in his brawny hand. Nevertheless, he held it while she brushed her hair and whisked on bright red lipstick.

While she worked, Seth glanced around as if hoping no one he knew saw them. Janna couldn't help smiling. He had nothing to worry about; they'd been jailed for half an hour and had yet to see anyone he knew.

He seemed relieved when she was finished and asked, "What are you going to do?"

"The only thing I can think of—flirt, just like Claudette Colbert in *It Happened One Night*."

Seth made a strangled sound. "You're going to hit on poor, innocent strangers and get them to bail us out?"

"Yes, unless you've come up with a better solution."

He held up his free hand and flicked it as if sending her on her way. "No. Carry on. I've got the feeling I'm going to see an expert at work. Maybe we should call all the store employees over here so they can pick up a few tips on selling."

Since she couldn't think of a snappy reply, she wrinkled her nose at him and faced the door once more. Little did he know. If she'd been more experienced and wordly-wise, she never would have gotten herself involved with Michael. And she certainly would have been able to make her father see that she was capable of handling her own life. She wasn't as experienced as she appeared, but she had inherited some acting ability from her mother, and she planned on using it.

When she saw a group of gangly teenage boys coming in the doors, she leaned across the top rail of the pen, batted her eyelashes, smiled invitingly, and said in a breathy voice, "Hello, boys. This may be your lucky day."

Beside her, Seth groaned.

CHAPTER TWO

TWENTY MINUTES LATER, their fine was paid and they were standing beside Seth's truck which one of the "deputies" had considerately driven to the store's parking lot. The two young men had shown up with more "criminals" in time to unlock the handcuffs that had trapped Seth and Janna together, apologizing profusely and thanking them for their cooperation.

Now, Janna could admit that it had been kind of fun. The starry-eyed boys she had accosted at the door had been willing to dig into their pockets and come up with the money she and Seth had needed. Seth had looked as if he wanted to sink through the floor, but their rescuers had been good-natured about the whole thing. She was glad to be out of there, though.

Outside, the temperature had cooled a bit since clouds had blown in, blocking the sun. Refreshed from being inside the air-conditioned store, Janna looked around at the place where she found herself.

It was a valley ringed by mountains. Across the road was a vast field of green plants. She assumed it was cotton, because Sue had told her that was the main crop grown in the valley that had been formed by the

Gila River. It wasn't such a bad place—at least when she wasn't on the verge of heatstroke.

Seth opened the truck, grabbed Janna's suitcase, which had been locked inside the cab, and tossed it into the truck bed. Janna tried not to wince even as she took hope from the gesture. His not dumping her suitcase out on the pavement was a good sign.

She cleared her throat and pushed her hair out of her face. Even though the sun was obscured by fat, fluffy clouds, in her silk outfit she was beginning to perspire again. "You said we'd talk." Apprehension set her heart hammering, but she forged ahead. "I got us out of there. Does it mean I have the job?"

Seth stared at her, then he took off his black Stetson and slapped it against his jeans. He ran his hands over his flattened hair. "Lady, you don't know when to quit, do you?"

"I should think you'd consider that a strong point in my favor. If I'd given up inside, we'd still be locked up."

"Which was your fault in the first place," he reminded her in what she considered to be a most ungentlemanly way. Apparently seeing hurt in her face, he sighed and said, "What are your qualifications?"

She had none, but she wasn't going to tell him that. Instead, she asked, "What were Sue's qualifications?"

He shrugged. "Years of domestic work, I guess. Emmie hired her because she knew Sue's mother once. She said Sue seemed quiet when they talked on the phone, be easy to have around."

Unlike a spoiled redhead from California wearing designer clothes, who opened her big mouth and got herself into a peck of trouble at every turn and flirted outrageously with impressionable young boys. Janna could almost hear his thoughts.

"You didn't answer my question about your qualifications. First off, can you cook?"

"That depends on what you mean by cooking," she hedged. The truth was she'd never cooked an actual meal, but she was a fabulous baker. Her mother's pastry chef had been the only one willing to teach her anything. But she reasoned that cooking couldn't be that hard to learn, could it?

As far as keeping house was concerned, she hadn't done much of that either, but how difficult could it be? She had watched the family housekeeper for years, and Janna knew she was at least as smart as Fiona Barron.

Seth's expression told her she'd better be more straightforward.

"I can cook some."

He closed his eyes as if praying for patience, then opened them again. "Listen, Janna..."

"I'm listening." She grinned, because she thought she could sense him wavering. Her eyes sparkled with merriment, though she couldn't have given a reason for it.

"This isn't funny."

Instantly, she sobered, but her eyes still danced. "Of course not."

Watching her, he didn't move for a few seconds, then he crossed his arms over his chest. His answering smile taunted her even as it attracted her. "You think you've got me over a barrel, don't you?"

"A girl can hope."

Sighing, he tugged at his ear. "I don't have much time to spend here. I had planned on picking Sue up, getting some supplies from the vet and heading home. Like I said, I've got a mare about to foal."

"It sounds like you're going to need me around your place."

"Not if you don't know how to work. What kinds of jobs have you had?"

Janna thought fast. Her job history was one subject she could be honest about, but it certainly didn't sound very impressive. There was something about this man, though, that told her she shouldn't tell him any lies, even a little one. She sensed a certain integrity in him that wouldn't take lies lightly.

"I have a degree in art education from the University of California, and I've worked the past three years as assistant manager of an art gallery. The gallery is closed temporarily for remodeling. The owner, Brian Feddoes, will be in his office. You can call him for a reference. He would give me a good one, but I'd appreciate it if you'd take my word for it."

"Are you running away from something?" He glanced pointedly at her left hand, which had so recently been handcuffed to his. "Your husband?"

Janna looked at the faint white line on her tanned finger where her engagement ring had once been.

She'd thrown it at Michael yesterday and had felt a tremendous upswelling of relief. "No. I'm not married."

"The cops, then? Is that why you surrendered to Laurel and Hardy back there?" He nodded in the direction of the bus depot.

"No! I've done nothing dishonest! Please believe me when I tell you that. I need to be on my own, and this job sounds like it would be perfect."

"What if you decide you can't handle it? I'm warning you, Janna, the Diamond B is a working ranch. There's no time for lying around, improving your suntan. In a couple of weeks your hands will look like they've never seen the inside of a nail salon."

Conscious of his scrutiny, Janna curled her fingertips into her palms. "I can do it," she repeated. "Give me a chance."

She didn't breathe while he was thinking it over. Finally, he gave a quick nod and said, "We'll give it a try." She saw something flicker in his incredibly dark eyes as he went on. "I know what it's like to have to prove yourself. You'll really be working for Emmie anyway, not for me. If you don't please her, out you go."

Relief and happiness washed over her. If she'd thought she could get away with it, she would have thrown her arms around his neck and hugged him. As it was, she grabbed his hand and pumped it enthusiastically. "Thank you. You don't know how much this means to me."

Seth didn't remove his hand from her grip, but his expression wasn't happy. "I don't know why you're running away. As long as you do your job, it's none of my business, but I've got a couple of young boys working for me, and I want you to be careful around them. There's not too many young women in Fawn Creek, and there's sure as hell none like you."

The joy faded from her face and she fought hard to control the irritation that had flared up as she dropped his hand. "I don't flirt with everyone who comes along."

"Only if you need to?"

"Well, yes, but you needed me to do it, and besides, it's harmless."

"Don't make a habit of it," he said gruffly.

Janna wondered briefly whether he was warning her off his hired hands—or himself. She nodded and felt as if the two of them had sealed a pact.

He held the truck door for her, but before she stepped inside, he stopped her. "Do you have anything else to wear? You'll be flirting with heatstroke if you ride in the truck in that outfit."

Janna glanced down at herself. "Oh, oh yes. I'll get something."

"*I'll* get something."

While she watched, he vaulted into the bed of his truck and flipped open her suitcase. He hunkered down beside it and began sifting through the contents.

Janna closed her eyes in mortification. A stranger was pawing her things. But she decided it wasn't enough of a problem to make an issue out of it.

Seth jumped down beside her after a few minutes with a pair of linen walking shorts and a white tank top. Despite her irritation with him, Janna took them gratefully and sailed into the ladies' room of the nearby fast-food place.

As she changed clothes in the tiny room, she told herself she should be more upset with his high-handedness, but it felt so good to get out of the yellow silk that she could forgive Seth Brody almost anything.

At the small sink, she washed the last of her makeup from her face, leaving her skin clean and shining and her freckles standing out like pale beacons. She fingered the gold necklace her mother had given her on her last birthday, wishing she could talk to her. Resolutely, she dropped the chain and reached for her shoulder bag. She was on her own now and couldn't depend on her mother to come rushing to her aid.

From the bag, she pulled a flowered scarf, which she tied around her neck. Finally she brushed her thick hair away from her face and wrapped an old elastic around it. Feeling immeasurably better, she gathered her discarded clothing, stuffed it into her bag and returned to Seth.

He was shifting impatiently from one foot to the other, but when she emerged, he gave her a quick, approving nod. "Now you look like something other than a Hollywood starlet. Let's go."

The statement surprised Janna but there didn't seem to be any hidden meaning to his words. She followed him out to the truck.

Janna cast him a sideways glance as she slid into the truck and slammed the door. She was looking forward to this job. It would be a relief to work around people who wanted nothing more from her than a strong back and willing hands. She'd had enough of people who only wanted to know her—or marry her—because of her family connections.

They left the small town behind and began winding through an area that Seth said was locally known as the Black Hills.

The rolling hills held few trees, but were dotted with dark green bushes that she recognized as cedars. The feathery light green ones were mesquite. There were also thick stands of prickly pear cactus, some of which still had their waxy yellow blossoms. She recognized stubby yuccas, the thin spikes of ocotillo cactus and spiny cholla, century plants with crepey white blossoms at the end of a single long stalk. Enthralled by the strange plants she'd seen only in pictures, she studied them as best she could from the speeding truck. The air coming in the open windows smelled fresh, with a hint of rain.

Before falling silent, Seth had told her that the ranch was more than an hour away.

Janna sneaked a glance at him. He was driving with one elbow propped on the open window and his long, work-roughened fingers lightly guiding the steering wheel. If she were to be as judgmental as he was being she would say that things came easily for him. The dented truck and faded jeans were mere camouflage. If he'd been driving a Rolls Royce and been wearing a three-piece suit, he couldn't have had more of an air of command.

She suspected that if he ever thought of himself at all, it would be with the knowledge that he pretty much did the best he could and didn't take himself too seriously.

After forty minutes, they had passed through the two small copper-mining towns of Clifton and Morenci and reached the base of the White Mountains. Seth turned off the highway onto a dirt road where they bumped and bounced along.

Due to an incoming mountain breeze and the rain clouds gathering behind them, the air grew suddenly cooler.

The country they were driving into was growing increasingly lush and beautiful. Junipers and twisted oaks gave way to pine and aspen as they traveled higher into the mountains.

On impulse, Janna hung her head out the window and breathed in the sharp, sweet smell of wet creosote rising from the areas where the rain had already hit. She took a deep, restorative breath and blissfully dropped her head against the seat back.

Through the open window, she could see mountains rising around them and across distant valleys, providing a misty foreground for the gathering clouds.

A pocket of mist moved toward them, forming a cloud. It condensed into a heavy mass with a swirling

underside that circled in the updraft for several minutes. A sudden breeze burst it apart. As the scattered
remnants dissipated, Janna laughed, delighted by the
place where she found herself. She turned to Seth who
took his attention from the road to look at her ques-
tioningly. "When I was a little girl, I wondered where
clouds went when they died." She held out her hands.
"This must be the place."

Seth's eyebrows rose in surprise and he tilted his
head as if seeing her from a new angle.

Embarrassed by her foolishness, Janna fluttered her
fingers nervously. "It's silly...." She cleared her throat
and smoothed the front of her tank top.

To her amazement, he laughed. Though she
couldn't tell if he was laughing with her or at her, she
enjoyed the deep, rich sound. She was pleased when he
became almost chatty. "The ranch is at a place called
Fawn Creek. Less than a dozen families live there.
Some are retired. Most are ranchers, like Emmie and
I, though some only come in on weekends and have
foremen to run the places for them. The rest are people who work for that copper mine we passed. They
maintain a water pumping station on the creek."

Janna glanced around at the wild beauty of the
place. "Do they mind being so isolated?"

Seth gave her a swift glance, then concentrated once
more on the road as he negotiated a series of hairpin
turns. "Some people do, so they don't stay around
long. The old families are used to it. Most of them
have lived and ranched here for years. The road into

town is almost always passable. We haven't had a landslide on this road in years.''

They took another curve, and Janna was treated to a view of a sheer drop of several hundred feet. She swallowed the lump that formed in her throat. ''I can't tell you how that comforts me.''

She heard him chuckle. Emboldened by their unspoken truce, she asked something that had been on her mind. ''Are you married? Do you have children?''

His hands clenched the steering wheel briefly. ''No. It's too rough on women up here.''

Flabbergasted by his chauvinistic attitude, Janna argued, ''But you said families live here. They must include women.''

''Well, those people have made their choices. I've made mine.''

His two clipped sentences effectively told her the subject was closed, but Janna couldn't let it drop. ''Your partner is a woman.'' She turned and lifted her left knee onto the worn seat. Propping her elbow on it, and her chin on her palm, she watched him as he drove.

''Wait 'til you meet her. Emmie is a law unto herself. She was born and raised here. She married her childhood sweetheart and worked on ranches in this area for years.''

''Then maybe it wasn't as hard on her as you think.''

Seth gave her an a-lot-you-know look that made her want to squirm, but he only said, ''Maybe.''

"What about you?" Janna persisted. "Have you lived here all your life?"

He glanced at her. "Has it occurred to you that you ask a lot more questions than you answer?"

Her cheeks reddened. "No, not really."

"Take it from me. You do." He paused as they rounded another tricky curve. "I was born here. The ranch had been in my family for about seventy-five years. My dad sold it to the Carrs when I was about seven and we moved to Phoenix. I bought into the ranch a couple of years ago after Emmie's husband died. She's eighty years old now, and she'll live the rest of her life at the ranch if she chooses. Then I'll be sole owner."

His brief and somewhat blunt story left her with a host of questions, but Janna suspected she wouldn't be getting any more information out of him. Besides, he was right. She was asking a lot more than she was answering.

Twenty bone-jarring minutes later, Seth turned the truck into a long, smoothly graded drive. Over the entrance was a neatly carved sign that said, Welcome to the Diamond B Ranch. Beside the lettering was a simple painting of a placid-faced bull.

Intrigued, Janna straightened. The drive forked a few yards up the hill. They took the left fork, which led up to the house. Off to the right, she could glimpse the roof of a large building, which she assumed was the barn. It was tucked under the slope of the hill. There were a few other outbuildings that appeared to be freshly painted.

Janna felt herself relax as she acknowledged she had been unconsciously worrying about what she was getting into. The dented and scratched state of Seth's truck appeared to be the exception rather than the rule at the Diamond B Ranch. Everything else that she could see was in good repair.

When they rounded the last stand of pine trees, the house was fully visible, and Janna's breath caught in her throat. The house was placed in commanding position on top of the hill and was flanked on one side by an orchard, and on the other, by a huge rose garden, riotous with color. Janna barely gave the orchard a glance as she concentrated on the house itself.

It was a massive rock building with two stories and a wraparound wooden porch that was painted a dark, brick red. An overgrown wild honeysuckle vine shaded one end of the porch. And from the rafters hung an old-fashioned swing, which was swaying gently as if its occupant had just left it.

Home. The thought and the feeling drifted over her as peacefully as the cloud she had watched forming, but it didn't disappear. In fact, it couldn't be shaken from her mind as Janna stared at the welcoming sight. A shiver passed through her at the strange certainty that filled her—this truly was home.

Seth stopped the truck beside the front gate, but Janna didn't move to get out. She merely turned in her seat as she continued to stare, transfixed, at the structure.

She didn't know what was wrong with her. She'd never reacted this way before. Having grown up in

Beverly Hills where style and size were everything, she couldn't actually articulate what was so attractive about this place. It was plain and unpretentious, but with such character. She had the perfectly ridiculous notion that any family who lived here would be happy, and any children born here would be well-bred and self-sufficient.

She loved it instantly with a fierce, unbreakable love.

"Janna? Miss Whitley, what's wrong?"

With a start, she realized Seth was standing by her door, and obviously this wasn't the first time he'd spoken to her. She blinked, then blushed and shook her head. She must be more exhausted than she thought if the sight of a comfortable house could send her into silly daydreams.

"Nothing," she replied, sliding out as he opened the door.

His lips quirked as he slammed it shut, grabbed her bag out of the truck bed, and then unlatched the gate for her. "Sorry if the place isn't to your liking, but as you said yourself, it's not for long." He motioned for her to precede him up the porch steps.

Appalled that he had so misunderstood her, Janna looked over her shoulder at him even as her steps carried her forward. "Now, wait a minute, you're wrong." She reached for the doorknob. In spite of her anxiety to correct Seth's misconception, she stopped to admire the entrance to the house. The heavy mahogany door had a stained glass panel down the middle that was as beautiful as anything Tiffany had ever created. It featured a cornucopia of fruit, spilling out in such jewel-like hues that Janna's mouth watered.

"Wrong about what?" Seth asked as he reached around to push open the door.

"About what I—" She ended in a gasp as she stepped inside and saw a woman lying at the base of the stairs.

CHAPTER THREE

SETH DROPPED JANNA'S BAG as they both dashed to the prone figure before them.

"Emmie, are you hurt?" Emotion shook Seth's voice as they knelt down beside her. His big, rough hands hesitated over the elderly woman as if he was afraid that, by touching her, he could do further damage.

Janna looked her over, noting she was tiny of stature, had snow white hair that stood up in a high crest around her head, and was dressed in a kelly green pants outfit. She lay on her side, with her right arm twisted under her. Her left foot was tangled in a small throw rug, telling Janna how the other woman had come to be lying on the floor.

Finally Seth reached for her free hand and sought out her pulse. "Emmie, talk to me. Are you all right?"

Emelyn Carr groaned, then cleared her throat. Her eyes, a deep blue, snapped open and she glared up at him. "Heck, no, I'm not all right. You think I'm taking a nap down here, boy?" Her voice was faint, but had an undercurrent of strength. When she shifted, Janna laid a hand on her shoulder to keep her still.

"Mrs. Carr, please don't move until we make sure you're not seriously hurt."

Those flashing blue eyes were turned on her and Janna felt as if she'd been pinned by a wrestler, so forceful was the other woman's personality. "Who're you? You're not Sue Perritt. I knew her mother. The woman was as broad as she was tall and had crossed eyes and a mustache, to boot."

In spite of her recent fright, Janna grinned. "No, ma'am, my name is Janna Whitley. I'll explain everything as soon as we see if you're okay."

"Ma'am, hmm? Well, at least you've been taught manners." She gave Seth another one of those fierce looks. "Let me up."

Seth, who had been gently testing the bones in Emmie's legs while this exchange was going on, said, "First I want to know where you're hurt."

She raised an eyebrow. "Seth, a blind man could see it's my right arm."

"Do you think it's broken?" He motioned for Janna to help him, and the two of them eased her onto her back.

"Nah, only a sprained wrist." Her words were brave, but her mouth was bracketed by white lines.

"We'll see about that." Seth slid both his arms under her and stood as if she weighed no more than a feather pillow. Janna scrambled up beside him. Carefully, she lifted Emmie's arm and laid it across her stomach, then followed as Seth carried the elderly woman toward the living room.

"This is what I get for trying to be a good host-ess," Emmie complained. "What took you so long?" She gave him a sly wink. "Didn't happen to see Me-linda Crandall, did you?"

"Yes, I did, but we'll save that story for later."

Obviously disappointed, Emmie sighed. "Anyway, I was waiting for you out on the porch swing. When I heard the truck, I came in to bring out the lemonade I'd made and slipped on that darned rug."

"I'm going to burn the damned thing," Seth mut-tered. Some color was beginning to return to his face, and his voice held the briskness Janna had already come to expect from him. She had been right in her guess that Mrs. Carr was probably his most vulnera-ble area. His affection for her was deep and genuine.

When Janna saw that he was headed toward an overstuffed couch, she hurried around him and ar-ranged the petit point pillows so Emmie could recline on them. As soon as Seth had her settled, Janna slid another pillow under the injured wrist. Emmie sucked in her breath in obvious pain, and Janna clucked sympathetically. "Mrs. Carr, I think it may be bro-ken."

"Nonsense, girl. I've had broken bones and I've had sprains and I darned sure know the difference. This is a sprain. And call me Emmie." She lifted her arm and tested the wrist. Immediately she gasped and returned it to the pillow.

Seth stepped backward, snatched his hat from his head and slammed it against his leg. "We're taking you into the clinic in Morenci to get it x-rayed."

"No, you're not. You're going to get me something stiff to immobilize it, as well as an elastic bandage. We'll wrap it up and if it's not better in the morning, you can take me to the clinic."

"I'll get what you need," Janna volunteered. "Just tell me where to find everything."

Seth looked apoplectic as he threw his hat into a nearby chair. "Emmie, you're the stubbornest woman in Greenlee County!"

"Of course I am. How do you think I lived to be this old?"

"Not by using good sense, that's for sure."

Seeing that this was going to degenerate into a full-blown argument, Janna held up her hand. "Why don't you two have this fight when Emmie's wrist is healed and she can put on her boxing gloves? Seth, she's hurt, and I don't think you're going to be able to talk her into having it x-rayed."

Her comment was met with a crack of laughter from Emmie and a glowering frown from Seth.

"That's what we need around here," Emmie crowed with satisfaction. "A woman who can talk back to King of the Hill, Seth Brody."

"We've already got one of those," he said, dryly.

"The bandages?" Janna prompted.

Seth told her to look in the downstairs bathroom near the kitchen. Janna hurried through the dining room and into the kitchen.

Though this would be her working area for the next few weeks, she barely glanced at the massive stove, big double refrigerator and acres of ceramic-tiled counter space. An inlaid wood tray with lemonade, three glasses and a bucket of ice sat on a long, polished oak table in the middle of the room.

She spied a narrow hallway leading to the back porch. The hall had two doors off of it. She opened the first and discovered a small bedroom that had a dresser, a nightstand with a vase of fresh red roses and a bed with a white pointelle bedspread. White eyelet curtains were puffed at the windows. It was obviously the room intended for Sue—the one Janna would now use. Although the room attracted her, she didn't linger, but turned to the other door. This was the bathroom, and she quickly found the necessary supplies. She rushed back to find that Emmie was beginning to regain a little of her color. Seth impatiently paced the floor, muttering that Emmie should see a doctor.

"Oh, go on and tend to Goldie. She needs you a lot more than I do." Emmie flapped her good hand at Seth, as Janna set down the first-aid supplies and began unrolling the elastic bandage. "This girl you've found can take care of me."

Janna smiled at her phrasing as she looked around for something to immobilize Emmie's wrist. She spied a stack of magazines in a basket beside a chair and went over to pick one up. To her horror, the one she had grabbed was a fashion magazine featuring a layout of famous mothers and their daughters. She and her mother had been included and were prominently displayed inside. Hastily, she buried it at the bottom of the stack and chose another one.

She turned around to see that Seth was giving both of them dark looks. "I'll be in for supper, and you'd better be feeling a lot better, or I'm taking you to the doctor no matter what you say." Having delivered the last word, he stalked out.

"He always wants to be sure everyone knows he's boss," Emmie said, sounding not the least bit intimidated. "Exactly like my Harry used to be. But if you've dealt with one bossy man, you know how to handle them all."

Janna thought of her father. She'd never learned how to handle him. "I'll have to take a few lessons from you while I'm here," she told her, gently slipping the magazine under Emmie's arm and lifting it so she could wrap it. She blessed the first-aid course she'd taken the winter before, as well as the number of minor cuts and scrapes she'd doctored for her two younger brothers.

"Why don't you turn that light on so you can see better?" Emmie nodded toward a nearby floor lamp.

Janna was surprised to see that the room was growing dark.

"Oh, I didn't realize it was so late."

"It isn't, but we're in a canyon here."

Janna did as she was told and returned to work. She could feel Emmie studying her while she finished her task. When the wrist was bandaged, she looked up, full of worry. "There you go. We'll need to soak it later and rebandage it. I still think you ought to have it x-rayed, though."

"We'll see. Right now I need some aspirin for the pain, and some ice to control the swelling."

"Oh, of course." Once again, Janna rushed out. She returned with two painkillers, a glass of water and a plastic bag full of ice.

Emmie popped the pills into her mouth, drank down the water, then handed the glass back to Jenna. Finally, she lifted her feet onto a hassock, rested the ice bag on her wrist and said, "Now, go get that tray of lemonade I left on the kitchen table, and we'll have a little talk. I'd like to know where Sue Perritt is . . . and why the daughter of a movie star and a millionaire is bouncing around the White Mountains with a devil like Seth Brody."

Though shocked by Emmie's question, Janna dutifully fetched the tray and poured out glasses of the icy beverage for both of them.

Janna stared down into her glass. "Are you going to tell Seth?"

"That depends."

"On what?"

"On why you're hiding from your family."

Janna rolled the glass back and forth between her palms. "How did you know who I am?"

"My one vice," Emmie said, indicating the stack of fashion magazines and newspaper tabloids. "I saw you bury that copy of *California Girl*."

"Oh." Janna couldn't think of anything else to say.

"I didn't make the connection at first," Emmie admitted. "My mind was a bit fuzzy."

Janna's eyes narrowed. "I don't believe your mind is *ever* fuzzy. I think you're a witch—or a leprechaun," she added, indicating the green pantsuit.

Emmie cackled with laughter. "I may be both. Now, start talking and don't leave out one juicy bit."

The older woman was undoubtedly feisty and outspoken, but she was also a good listener. If Janna had detected even a hint of the morbid curiosity she and her family so often faced, she wouldn't have said anything. Instead, she sensed sympathy and understanding behind Emmie's wisecracking exterior, so she told her the whole story.

When she was finished, Emmie tilted her head to one side like an inquisitive bird and asked, "Why did your father hire this Michael Barrington to marry you?"

Janna rolled her eyes. "Heaven only knows. Dad wants to be sure my brothers and I don't make the mistakes he made. He inherited a fortune and squandered it before he was twenty-five, then had to start over again from scratch. I've dated two different artists in the past couple of years. Not seriously, but Dad was afraid I might marry one of them and then regret it."

"And he didn't think you'd regret marrying this Michael?"

"Not if Michael had managed to keep romancing me the way he'd done for the past two months. He swept me off my feet so fast I hardly knew what was happening. He said and did all the right things."

Emmie shook her head. "Marriage isn't like that, I'm afraid. If you don't really love someone, you don't feel like continuing to romance them."

Janna's lips twisted ruefully. "Obviously, Michael didn't love me since he decided to try his technique on someone else."

"Where was your mother while all this was going on?"

"She's on a movie location in Kenya. She's been gone a month and probably won't be home for another two weeks." Janna's heart spasmed at the thought. She needed to have a good, long talk with her mother, but feared if she let Shea intervene, her father would think of it as a sign of weakness. She had to stand up for herself and go it alone.

When Emmie was silent for a long time, Janna said contritely, "I'm sorry. Here you are in pain, and I've burdened you with my problems."

"Nonsense. If I hadn't wanted to know, I wouldn't have asked." Emmie used her good hand to reach over and squeeze Janna's knee. "But good Lord, girl, this is better than a soap opera. So what you're looking for is a place where you can prove yourself *and* heal your heart before confronting your father?"

"That pretty well sums it up."

"It may take longer than a couple of weeks."

"Nevertheless, that's all I've got. Sue will most likely be well by then and want her job."

Emmie surveyed Janna for a long moment. "You know, I think we *will* go into Safford tomorrow. We'll have someone examine my wrist, see how Sue is doing, and then we'll go visit Edith Collins, a friend of mine. Her grandsons are working here on the ranch this summer and she's a little lonely. I think she'd be willing to have Sue stay with her when she leaves the hospital. That way, Sue will be cared for, and you'll have a place to hide out longer if you need to."

Janna blinked. "But I'm a stranger. Why would you do that for me?"

"It's not just for you, honey. Don't get me wrong." Emmie sobered suddenly, her softly lined face looking every year of her age. "The work here is hard. We need someone strong and healthy to help out. Sue won't be up to any heavy work for at least six weeks, maybe longer. I hired her because I knew her mother, a workhorse if there ever was one, and I'm betting Sue's like her."

Janna smiled, then shrugged. "I can't say. We talked quite a bit, and she seemed very levelheaded and practical, but then she got so sick...."

Emmie indicated her bandaged wrist. "And you're probably fed up with dealing with sick people."

"Oh, no, not in the least," Janna denied.

Emmie laughed. "Well, you'll have a change of pace anyhow. I know you're exhausted. I can see it in your eyes. But you'll have to get dinner for Seth and the hands. I can't do it." She winced as she moved her wrist. "I've got to lie down and keep ice on this thing. I can already tell that the swelling's going to get worse before it gets better."

Janna stood up hastily and glanced at the ornate clock that stood on the wide oak mantel. "Fine. Tell me what to do."

Emmie blinked. "*Tell* you? You don't mean you can't cook!"

Sheepishly, Janna shrugged. "I'm a great baker, though. François, my mother's pastry chef, taught me. I make a killer lemon meringue pie."

Emmie shook her head as she got to her feet. Holding her wrist close to her chest, she said, "You'd better make several. It's Seth's favorite, and if you mess up dinner, you'll need something to sweeten him up. There's plenty of canned food in the pantry closet and a freezer full of stuff on the back porch. Help yourself to whatever you need. Also, there's every kind of kitchen tool, appliance and gadget you can imagine in there. Seth buys 'em. He's crazy about gadgets."

Janna shifted uncomfortably. "Emmie, exactly how many people will I be cooking for?"

"Including you, me and Seth? We've got four hands here this summer and occasionally there's a neighbor here at suppertime. I'd say seven or eight to supper."

Seven or eight! Her answer nearly sent Janna reeling. What had she gotten herself into? As she waited for her heart to stop clogging her throat, Janna assisted Emmie upstairs to bed, freshened the bag of ice for her wrist, then made her way back to the kitchen. Emmie was right. There was a state-of-the-art food processer that had more attachments than a Swiss Army knife, but Janna didn't even consider using the thing. She wouldn't know where to start.

It took her quite a while to find the ingredients she needed for the pies and to figure out how to work the range and oven, but once the pies were done, they were beautiful, tart-sweet and topped with golden meringue.

She set them to cool on the countertop and then surveyed the contents of the pantry and freezer. As Emmie had promised, there was a wide variety of goods, but nothing that could simply be popped into a microwave. Besides, the microwave looked as if she'd need an engineering degree to figure out how it worked.

Exhausted, Janna rubbed her hand across her face and wondered if she could get a pizza parlor to deliver to the middle of nowhere. Nah, it would have to come by parachute drop, and she didn't think any pizza parlor was desperate enough to try that gimmick.

She was determined not to feel sorry for herself and to remember that she had gotten herself into this. Now she had to deal with it. The whole point of leaving home had been to prove herself, but cooking for seven—maybe eight! Grimly, she grabbed several cans of chili and some crackers from the pantry. She heated the chili, slowly so as not to scorch it, and arranged the crackers attractively on a plate. As an afterthought, she added slices of cheese. Next, she scraped carrots, cut them into sticks and grated more cheese to top the bowls of chili.

She thought longingly of the way S. Z. Sakall had done the cooking, and Barbara Stanwyck had passed it off as her own in *Christmas in Connecticut*. Only Janna didn't have anyone to bail her out, so she did what she could.

She was pouring lemonade into tall glasses when footsteps sounded on the porch. Seth followed three men into the hallway and waited his turn to wash up in what she was beginning to think of as *her* bathroom.

As soon as she had heard them coming, Janna had whipped off her apron. Now, she ran smoothing fingers over her hair and fluffed her bangs, which had begun tightening into ringlets from the heat of the stove.

Seth paused by the bathroom door and stared across the space of the kitchen at her. He glanced from the wild thickness of her auburn hair, down to her toes, then up again, finally settling on her flushed face.

Something flickered in his eyes. It made heat run beneath the surface of Janna's skin. She shivered, and her lips trembled into a smile. At the sight of it, Seth frowned and shouldered his way into the bathroom as two of the others were coming out. Within a few minutes, the four of them were trooping into the kitchen.

Seth seemed to have forgotten the strange moment, and Janna blinked, struggling to keep up with his changing moods. Seth asked after Emmie, then introduced the two youngest men as Steve and Gus Collins. "Their grandmother is Emmie's best friend," Seth explained. "So the boys are working with us this summer to see what life is like on a ranch."

Janna remembered the friend Emmie had mentioned and wondered how Seth felt about getting stuck with a couple of greenhorns—three, now that she had come.

Gus and Steve were blond and sunburned and their kinship was unmistakable. They were taller than Seth, with the bony, underdeveloped appearance of most boys their age. She guessed that, like her brothers, they were hollow clear down to their dusty boots.

The other man smiled and nodded as introductions were made. José was an elderly Hispanic man with expressive brown eyes and a soft voice. Like the Collins boys, he eyed the pot of chili hungrily as the three of them pulled out chairs and sat down.

Not so their boss. Seth surveyed the table with a frown. "Janna, could I speak to you outside for a minute?"

Her nervous, welcoming smile faded. "Okay."

He headed for the porch, and she reluctantly trudged after him.

Once there, he turned and looked down at her. "When you said you could cook 'some,' is this what you meant? Heating things up?"

She caught her bottom lip between her teeth. This was the moment she had been dreading, but she couldn't lie. "Yes."

"Tell me, are you and truth total strangers?"

She ran her thumb and forefinger over the chain at her throat. She couldn't quite look him in the eye. "We've met."

"Obviously a passing acquaintance."

"I knew you wouldn't hire me if I told you the truth."

"Damned right."

"I can bake, though, and I should be able to learn what I need to know—"

"You can bake, but you can't cook? That's ridiculous."

"Oh, no it isn't, I... Wait here." Janna whipped around and stalked back to the kitchen, ignoring the ranch hands who watched her with great interest.

Janna took a knife from a drawer, cut out a piece of lemon pie, slapped it onto a plate with no regard for neatness, grabbed a fork and carried it back to Seth. With her eyes full of challenge, she impaled a piece with the fork and held it an inch from his lips. "Here. Taste this."

Seth gave her a black look, but realizing he could do nothing but accept the bite—unless he wanted to wear it on his chin—he opened his mouth and let her slip the fork in as if she was feeding a stubborn baby.

When she withdrew the fork, his hand shot up to grab her wrist. He held it, suspended in the air, while he chewed, swallowed and considered.

With one hand holding the plate and the other caught in Seth's grip, Janna felt trapped while she awaited his verdict. He made a gentle noise of surprise deep in his throat and said, "I'll be damned, it's not half-bad."

She twisted her hand from his grasp and gave him a triumphant smile. "It's bloody wonderful." François had taught her well, and she knew it.

Seth raised his brows. "You know, your subservient attitude still needs work, Janna."

She felt her face heating, but fought not to answer back.

"You still can't cook."

She waggled the plate at him. "This proves I can learn."

"Save it." Seth ran his hand over his hair. "I made a big mistake bringing you here. A tenderfoot like you doesn't fit in."

Stung, Janna started to protest, but he held up his hand to stop her. He looked tired and frustrated, leaving Janna feeling guilty about being the cause of at least part of it. "Well, you're here now, and Emmie can't help you. It hardly seems worth all the effort since you'll only be here a short time, but how about if I teach you to cook steaks tomorrow?"

She hid her hurt and blessed him with a grateful smile. "That would be wonderful. I'll learn fast. I know I can do it."

"How many times have I heard that today?"

Her gratitude faded. "Now, wait a—"

She was interrupted by the pounding of boots. Another ranch hand climbed the back steps to the porch and slammed his way inside. He was tall and gangly and revealed a bald head when he removed his hat. "Seth, you'd better go see to Goldie. I think her foal's hung up. She's really struggling."

Seth turned immediately. "Thanks, Barker. I'll go right now." He gestured toward the kitchen. "Why don't you stay and eat? When you're finished, take the boys and check on the south pasture gate. I noticed it was hanging crooked when I came home this afternoon. That new bull probably tried to jump it.''

He gave Janna one final glance that told her what he thought of the dinner she'd prepared, then headed out the door. Not willing to let their discussion drop, she set the plate down on top of a cabinet by the back door and went after him. He took off at a lope, his long legs covering the ground in incredible strides. Janna had to sprint to keep up. She stumbled on the rough ground, though, and by the time she recovered her balance, he was past the bunkhouse and outbuildings and in the barn.

Janna rushed inside the barn and was assaulted by new and unusual smells: the not unpleasant ones of hay, dust, and well-kept animals. There were various implements and tools hanging neatly on wall hooks. To one side, there was a stack of hay bales. On the top, surveying his surroundings like a king on his throne, sat the biggest calico cat Janna had ever seen. Near the back of the building was a series of stalls. From one of these, she heard a low, distressed whinny.

Seth was kneeling in the stall and glanced up when he saw her. ''I know you probably followed me down here to argue, but why don't you make yourself useful?''

''Doing what?'' she asked, moving forward. Reluctance dragged at her feet. She had never seen an animal born and wasn't too sure she wanted to now. Nevertheless, Janna peeked over the railing and saw that the mare was lying down.

Goldie lived up to her name. She was a gorgeous palomino with a coat of pale gold and a mane that was almost platinum.

Janna, who had been afraid of horses as a child, saw nothing to fear in this poor, suffering creature.

Seth went into the tack room and removed his shirt to display a formidably attractive chest and a flat, hair-dusted stomach. Janna told herself she shouldn't notice such things about her boss, but it did no good. As she watched, Seth scrubbed his hands and arms, then dried himself carefully. Carrying a big stack of clean rags, he returned to Goldie. He talked slowly and quietly as he crouched beside her.

The mare tossed her head and rolled pain-filled eyes as he checked the position of her foal. Watching, Janna winced and turned her face away.

"What are you cringing for?" Seth asked. "Goldie's the one in pain."

"I'm being empathetic."

"I'm sure she appreciates it." He withdrew his hand. "Have you ever seen an animal born before?"

"I saw *Heartland* with Rip Torn and Conchata Ferrell. In the last scene they help a cow give birth. It was disgusting."

"Then what are you doing here?"

"Proving myself to yet another man," she answered testily.

He smiled a mocking smile. "Is that right? Well, then come and help me."

Janna stared, mouth agape, pale green eyes wide. "Me?"

"Sure. You wanted a job on a ranch, didn't you?" The way he raised his eyebrows told her he expected her to refuse. Perversely, she decided she could do it if he could.

Chin up, she stepped into the stall and knelt beside the prostrate horse. She let out a long breath as she placed a hand on Goldie's lush mane. "What should I do?"

She was sure her exhausted eyes were playing tricks on her when she saw a hint of respect in his face.

"Hold her head and talk to her. I'll have to pull the foal."

Janna wasn't quite sure what he meant by that until he disappeared into the tack room and returned with a block and tackle. He looped the shackle end over a large hook on the wall and drew out a length of rope.

Janna paled. "What are you going to do with that?"

He didn't even spare her a glance. "The foal's supposed to come out forefeet first with his head tucked between them. This one's not only an exceptionally big foal, but he's got his head turned back over his shoulder. If I don't help, he and Goldie will both die." Seth made a loop on one end of the rope and reached inside the struggling horse with it. To her credit, Janna didn't gag.

Before he began to pull, he looked up at Janna's ashen face. "Talk to her. It'll give you both something to concentrate on," he said with a hint of sympathy in his voice.

Janna marveled at the wealth of knowledge, experience and courage he needed in his job. Life was too hard, the margin for error too broad, and the possibilities of failing in the livestock industry too great. Even something as natural as a mare giving birth could be fraught with risks. Seth took them, though. There was no choice. With no more delays, Seth grasped the rope dangling from the block and tackle and began pulling, slowly and carefully. Fascinated, Janna watched his back and arm muscles bunch and ripple with the effort. Her throat went uncomfortably dry, and she felt odd shivers of pleasure deep inside.

Appalled at herself, she averted her gaze and gave Goldie a hug, offering her the comfort of one female to another. Her initial reluctance gave way to sympathy and fascination as she watched the mare's great muscles expand and contract. Suddenly, Goldie lifted herself from her bed of hay. She gave a great, wrenching whinny, her sides heaved, and her foal slithered into the world. "Oh!" Janna shouted in surprise and wonder at sight of the dark, wet newborn. "It's beautiful," she breathed as Seth grabbed one of the towels he had brought from the tack room and began rubbing mucus from the foal's nose and mouth. "Is it a boy or a girl?"

He flashed her a grin. "It's a filly, a girl." When he looked down again, his grin faded.

When he didn't say anything, Janna prompted him. "Is she okay?"

"I don't think so."

"What's wrong?"

"Neck was twisted in the birth canal."

Janna scooted closer. "So?"

He had a bleak expression on his face. "So if we can't straighten it out, she'll die."

Janna swallowed. "How do we do that?" She couldn't have said exactly when she'd stopped thinking of herself as an observer and become a participant. The foal was lying on its side, its head at an odd angle. There was an indentation at the back of her neck that moved when she struggled for breath.

"I don't know, but right now I've got to let Goldie get acquainted with her daughter."

Goldie had turned her head to get a better view of her baby, then tried getting to her feet. After a few tries, she succeeded and began licking her newborn. A few minutes later, Seth gently drew her away and put her in another stall. She whinnied in protest.

"I'm not sure how we straighten out her neck. I've never done it before. José might know. Go get him, will you?" She jumped up and started to leave, then spun around as a thought struck her. "If it's her neck, couldn't you put it into place?"

"Sure, if I knew how."

Janna rubbed her knuckles along her jaw. "I used to date a chiropractor."

Seth rolled his eyes. "My great-uncle was married to a fan dancer, but that's got nothing to do with this, either."

Janna moved to stand beside him. "What I'm saying does have something to do with this."

He turned to stare at her in amazement. "You're saying we should take this filly to a chiropractor?"

CHAPTER FOUR

"THAT'S EXACTLY WHAT I'm saying. A chiropractor works on the spine, doesn't he?"

"There's two things wrong with that idea." Seth held two fingers up an inch from her nose. "First, it's a crazy idea, and second, the closest one's an hour away. And third—"

"You said two things were wrong with my idea."

"Third, it's another of your harebrained schemes, like taking a job that's not right for you and getting us jailed today."

Janna crossed her arms at her waist. "I never have harebrained schemes. I admit that sometimes my ideas aren't well thought out, but . . ."

"I rest my case."

She thought she recognized the reluctance for what it was and gave him a shrewd look. "Besides, if anyone heard about you taking a horse to a chiropractor, you might be laughed out of the cattleman's association, right?"

He didn't answer, but his face and stance were full of frustration. "If you're not going to get José, I will."

The barn door creaked softly on its hinges. "There's no need. I'm here." The wiry little man walked up behind them and glanced down at the foal, then knelt to examine her. Distressed, he shook his head. "It's bad, *muchacho*."

"I know," Seth answered, his dark eyes mirroring his concern over the foal's condition. "Can you help her?"

"No. I've seen them with twisted necks, but never this bad. I would hurt her more than I would help."

"I have an idea that might work," Janna said boldly, ignoring Seth's derisive snort. She told José her suggestion.

When José nodded, Seth was incredulous. "You don't think that could work, do you?"

"Why not?" José asked, earning Janna's undying gratitude.

"We can at least try. We can't just let the poor thing suffer." She looked down at the filly whose big eyes were rolling in fear. Behind them, Goldie kept up her frantic cries at being separated from her baby.

Seth threw his hands in the air. "All right, all right. I agree something has to be done, but it would take us more than an hour to get her into town, and the doctor's office would be closed."

"Do you know Mrs. Berk?" José asked, rubbing his stubbly chin.

"Sure, she and her husband retired here a couple of years ago. I met them at a barbecue last summer."

"I hear she was a chiropractor in Tucson."

"Then she could help us?" Janna put her hand on Seth's arm.

She waited while he thought it over, knowing this wasn't a good time to push him. She feared he was going to refuse, but when the newborn made another of its strangled sounds, he nodded his head. "José, call and tell her we're on our way over."

Janna managed to swallow her shout of triumph as José hurried out. Seth got a blanket from the tack room and wrapped the filly in it. He lifted her into his arms and started toward the door, speaking to Janna as he passed. "Since this was your idea, you can come along."

"Gladly." Janna stopped to give the restless mare a reassuring pat. "We'll bring your daughter right back," she whispered, then scurried into the dark barnyard after Seth. She jumped into the truck and held out her arms for the newborn.

As he laid the foal in her arms, he said, "Be sure to support her head."

Janna smiled briefly, thinking that he sounded as if he was handing her a newborn baby rather than a horse. She had to admire his flexibility. He might think this was a harebrained idea, but at least he was will-ing to try it. He climbed into the truck and within moments they were wheeling out of the yard.

Once they reached the rough main road, Janna had a hard time hanging onto the filly, who was fright-ened by the truck and the bumpy ride. When she tried to lift her head, Janna gently pushed it back down. Then she started kicking out with her long, skinny legs, hitting the dashboard. Fearful that the filly would hurt herself, Janna frantically tried to capture the tiny, flailing hooves. It was impossible. As soon as she got one end under control, the other went wild.

"Umph," she grunted as her small patient lifted her head and clipped Janna under the chin. "This is like trying to stuff a fat lady into a girdle—something's always popping out."

Seth gave a surprised chuckle as he glanced at her slim frame, visible in the greenish glow of the dash-lights. "What would you know about that?"

"I worked one summer on a movie set, helping the wardrobe lady," she said, then feared she'd said too much. The movie had been one of her mother's.

"Oh, yeah? Meet anybody famous?"

She shifted uncomfortably, wishing she'd kept her mouth shut. "Not really. Most of the cast were un-knowns. Still are." Except for her mother.

The foal made another lunge, and Janna tried to soothe her as she waited for his next question, pray-ing she wouldn't have to lie.

To her relief, he suggested, "Why don't you move over here? I can drive with one hand and keep her head down with the other. You can hold her hooves."

Grateful for the help, Janna did as he suggested, sliding across the bench seat so that they were touch-ing thigh to thigh. After a few moments of maneuver-ing, Seth laid his arm along the foal's neck and cupped the side of her head with his hand.

The filly quieted immediately, as if sensing she was safe. Janna looked at Seth with new respect. He glanced over at her and grinned. "You don't have to look like you've just seen Mr. Hyde turn into Dr. Jekyll."

"I guess you just have to have a certain touch."

"Or a lot of experience."

The cab of the truck seemed to have shrunk, making the interior warm and intimate. His biceps were pressed to her shoulder and felt as solid as a brick wall. Janna had the crazy notion that she could have leaned against it forever and felt as safe as the horse did. The thought had her wanting to shift away, but she couldn't without disturbing the filly.

Over the animal's raspy breathing, Janna was sure she could hear the pounding of her heart, which had increased its rate for no apparent reason. She didn't know what to do about such a reaction because it was completely inappropriate and badly timed. She wondered if she was quite as indifferent to the whole male gender as she wanted to be. Or maybe it was just this one. She didn't like that thought at all. Janna lifted her hand from the filly's flank and rubbed her eyes. Obviously, she was experiencing some kind of exhaustion-induced hallucinations. When she caught Seth studying her, she dropped her hand.

Within a few minutes, they had pulled into the yard of a neat little house close to the road. The light over the front door came on as Seth brought the truck to a stop. A man and woman walked out onto the porch. They were smiling quizzically as Seth carried the foal up the steps, with Janna walking carefully beside him, holding the filly's head.

"Good evening, Mrs. Berk," Seth greeted and nodded to her husband. "I'm grateful that you're willing to help us out." Janna had to admire the way he said it, with no hint that he believed it was a crazy idea.

"I'll admit, this is going to be a first for me." Mrs. Berk said dryly as she pointed to a long, wide bench. "Put her down right there."

"Can you help her?" Janna asked anxiously, hovering nearby.

"Can't tell yet." She pulled away the blanket and ran her hands over the foal's neck, pausing at the obvious indentation. The horse jerked and would have squealed if she'd had the breath. "Hmm, pushing on the windpipe. Yes, I can help."

With that, she knelt beside the bench, pressed her knuckles into the back of the foal's neck and twisted the head. The horse gave a tiny scream of protest, then quieted as her breathing eased. Her eyes rolled, but they no longer looked terrified.

Janna gave a hoot of satisfaction, and Seth grunted with surprised relief. It was then that she realized she was clutching his hand hard enough to cut off the circulation. She let go of his fingers as if they had suddenly become red-hot, wondering when she had grabbed him.

He didn't seem to notice as he thanked Mrs. Berk, who refused any payment and laughed over her triumph. "I'm going to write this up for a professional journal. They'll never believe it."

Elated, Janna and Seth headed home. Within minutes, the foal had been reunited with Goldie, who smelled her all over, before licking her again. The foal settled down to nurse a little while later as her two rescuers watched.

"She's so pretty," Janna said dreamily, propping her arms on the top rail of the stall and resting her chin on her hands. "You should call her Silver."

"Heigh-ho, Silver, away," Seth snorted derisively. "I think you've seen too many old movies."

"A person can never see too many old movies. Besides, it's a good name."

He lifted his hands in surrender. "Okay. Silver, it is."

Satisfied, Janna went back to watching the foal. When she seemed to be swallowing with no difficulty, Seth motioned toward the door. They headed back to the house.

"I owe you an apology," Seth began as they strolled through the cool night air.

"Apology accepted," Janna answered with a smug grin.

"Don't think that all problems here can be solved that easily."

"I don't. But I'm willing to take each problem as it comes, one at a time."

"Janna, around here, problems don't line up and wait their turn. Mostly, they all try to crowd through the gate at once."

"I can handle it."

He studied her in the glow of the yard light. "I hope that's self-confidence speaking, not foolhardiness."

"All you can do is wait and see."

"Maybe you're right." His eyes narrowed as he regarded her. "I think you've surprised me."

With a soft laugh, she tilted her head. "You *think* I have?"

"You've had a lot thrown at you today, and you held up better than I thought you would."

Her proud smile collapsed when he continued, "Too damned bad you can't cook." He held up his hand when she started to speak. "I know, I know. You can learn. I just hope we don't all die of indigestion first."

Flushing with irritation, she put her hands onto her hips and faced him. "Yesterday, I broke my engagement, had a fight with my father and left home. Today, I checked someone into a hospital, got the two of us out of a jail-a-thon, bandaged a sprained wrist and cooked dinner for seven people. Not to mention helping to save a newborn foal."

When she finished speaking, she could see grudging admiration come into Seth's face. "You're well on your way to proving yourself, aren't you?"

"Yes." Janna reached up to run her hand across her eyes as exhaustion swamped her.

His straight, full lips twitched. "Well, I guess your next challenge will be gathering eggs and milking the cow."

JANNA STRUGGLED out of bed when the alarm on the spooled maple nightstand went off. She blinked at the clock and grumbled, "I didn't even know those numbers existed in relation to morning." Then she yawned, pulled on her robe and stumbled across the hall to the shower.

She decided to wear shorts and a white T-shirt, even though the morning was cool. It would surely be hot later. Over the T-shirt, she put on a loose camp shirt of tomato red Calcutta cloth and tied the tails above her waist. Lastly, her hand fell on her bottle of perfume. It did, indeed, cost two hundred dollars an ounce and had been a gift from her mother. She considered not wearing any, but then defiantly sprayed some on. Let Seth Brody think whatever he wanted.

By the time she was dressed, she was beginning to wake up enough to make plans for the day.

Seth's statement about milking and gathering eggs had nearly sent her to her knees, but as usual, she'd assured him she could do it. His answer had been nothing short of a guffaw. She was determined to prove him wrong.

And that meant she had to have those two chores done *and* breakfast ready by the time Seth came downstairs.

She slipped on her sandals and went into the kitchen to find something in which to gather eggs. There, she saw a large silver bucket sitting on the counter. It hadn't been there last night. She knew because she had dragged herself into the kitchen on her way to check on Emmie. She had expected to find the place as messy as she had left it. Instead, it had been spotless. She wondered if José and the Collins boys had cleaned it.

Seth had gone in with her to see Emmie, who had been sleeping fitfully, then he had raided the refrigerator, eating the last of the chili and almost an entire pie while she had staggered off to bed. Now she glanced at the dishes Seth had rinsed and left in the sink, then at the bucket. It, too, had been recently rinsed. On a hunch, she looked in the refrigerator and saw a pitcher of milk, still foamy on top. Someone had done the milking, but she could still gather eggs. It shouldn't be too hard. After all, she'd seen Claudette Colbert do it in *The Egg and I* at least ten times.

On the back porch, she discovered a basket with a few tiny feathers stuck to it and decided that it must be the egg-gathering basket. With it swinging jauntily from her arm, she bounced down the back steps and out into the yard.

The big calico cat and the two collies were eating from pans beside the porch steps. Janna stopped to pet them, then continued down the hill to the chicken coop beside the barn.

She tried to unlatch the gate, but it was hanging slightly crooked. She had to use both hands—one to lift the gate, the other to open the latch. This was the first thing she'd seen on the Diamond B Ranch that wasn't in tiptop shape. It gave her hope that Seth wasn't quite as much of a perfectionist as she had feared.

She stepped inside the small yard, and then into the coop itself. Cautiously, she looked around. Some of the hens had left their nests to scratch and peck in the dirt. Others were still on their nests. Janna didn't know if she was supposed to walk up and sneak her hand under the setting hens, or shoo them off the nest, but decided to try the gentle approach first.

Sidling up to the shelf on which the nests had been built, she was delighted to discover eggs in several of the henless ones. She placed them carefully in the basket and came to the first setting hen, who seemed to be asleep. Her fingers had barely touched the nest when the hen turned and pecked at her hand.

"Oh!" She snatched it away and stood glaring at the hen, whose beady red eyes glared right back.

Knowing that discretion was the better part of valor, she moved on to the next occupied nest. Here, the hen didn't seem to mind if Janna took every egg in the place, nor did the one after that. Her confidence buoyed, Janna finished and looked into her basket with all the reverence of one viewing the crown jewels. She had ten eggs and would be done once she took the egg from the belligerent hen.

She would make up for last night's dinner by preparing crepes for breakfast, just the way François had taught her.

Surreptitiously, she stepped up to the nest, moving her hand slowly toward the shelf. Just as she'd reached the nest, the hen whipped its head around and nailed her, drawing blood.

"Oh, you miserable featherbrain," Janna cried, cradling her hand. "I'm going to get that egg. It won't do you any good. It'll just rot if you keep it."

Deciding that a distraction might be in order, she looked around. If she could get the hen to look somewhere else, she could get that egg. She found a handful of straw on the plank floor and tossed it onto the shelf beside the nest.

The chicken erupted off the shelf as if she'd been stung by a yellow jacket. Squawking, she flew straight at Janna's head, knocking her backward. Trying to protect herself, Janna threw up her hands. Eggs hit her head and shoulders, others splattered on the wall behind her. Two even landed on her feet.

"My eggs!"

The other chickens added to the mayhem. They all left their nests at once. Their limited flying ability was just enough to get them off the roost and into Janna's hair. She batted at them and within moments the entire flock was hopping frantically about the floor.

The hen who had caused all the trouble was once again on the attack. This time the brunt of her rage was focused on Janna's toes.

"Yeow!" Dancing on one foot, then the other, Janna whirled toward the door, not seeing the tall figure that had just appeared there.

"What the— Oomph!" Seth staggered as she slammed into him. His hands shot out, grabbing her waist to steady her, but she twisted out of his grasp, trying to escape the vengeful beak. "Janna, stand still, that stupid chicken's not going to hurt you."

She gave him a wild look. "Are you kidding? She's out for blood."

"Now calm down, and I'll—"

"Watch out!" Several of the other birds had decided to join the battle. Flapping and squawking, they zeroed in on Janna's toes. She jumped behind Seth, shoving her feet as close to his as possible. She wrapped her arms around his waist and squeezed. Then she buried her chin against his back as she peeked around him to keep a wary eye on her tormenters.

"Janna, good Lord, what are you doing?" He staggered backward, but she wouldn't let go. Instead, she moved her feet with his so the chickens couldn't get her. Thrown off-balance by having her plastered to his back, he slipped in the broken eggs, almost sending them both onto the floor. He reached behind himself to steady her, then lurching drunkenly, he got them out to the tiny yard.

"Janna," he grunted, "let me go."

"No! They'll peck me again."

"I can't get the gate. You'll have to do it."

"Oh, okay." She looked up and gingerly turned around. The chickens were still squawking and flapping about, apparently proud of having driven out the intruders. Seth shielded her as she pulled and tugged at the latch.

When she couldn't get it loose, Seth asked in exasperation, "Wouldn't it be easier if I did it?"

"No," she squeaked. "You stay between me and those miserable birds."

Using both hands, she finally managed to get the gate open, and they stumbled through. Inside the pen, the chickens placidly fluffed their feathers and began pecking at the ground.

"Are you all right?" Seth asked, pulling her into his arms.

"I'm fine." Now that the fright was over, Janna was mortified. "They were all coming at me at the same time and pecking my feet...."

Seth linked his hands at the back of her waist and looked down at her. "That's Jackhammer's first line of defense. She hates toes for some reason."

"Now you tell me." Janna felt something damp on her cheek and rubbed her face on her shoulder to wipe it off. Glancing down, she saw that it was egg yolk and wondered how much more she was wearing. She leaned back and saw that it was smeared down the front of her shirt. She could also see that she'd transferred a great deal of it to Seth's brown plaid work shirt. She sighed.

"I didn't know you were going to act like Rebecca of Sunnybrook Farm and go out gathering eggs this morning."

"You *told* me to."

He had the grace to look ashamed. "I guess I should have told you I was just kidding. I intended to do it myself today and teach you how later."

"Well, it's later. You'd better teach me now." She wiggled slightly. "You can let go of me now," she said pointedly when his grip didn't loosen.

"Oh, I don't know." His dark eyes gleamed devilishly. "This is very pleasant. I can't remember ever having a woman throw herself at me—especially not one needing to be rescued from chickens."

"I know it's stupid to be afraid of them, and…and I'm not really… I just can't stand things flying at me." As she babbled out this explanation, Janna was looking everywhere but at him. She was uncomfortably aware of the strength of the arms and hands that were holding her against him.

Seth glanced down at her mouth, then up into her eyes. When he spoke, his voice was hoarse and he had to clear his throat and start again. "Janna?"

She finally looked at him. "Yes?"

"You don't have to be perfect at everything the first day." His voice was a husky murmur.

"Well, that's good to know because I'm sure I can do—"

"Janna?"

"Hmm?"

"Shut up." Then he did the shutting up for her by putting his mouth over hers and kissing her.

At first, Janna was too shocked by the unexpected caress to respond. She'd been resting her hands on his biceps and was just gathering her strength to push him away when the wonder of his warmth and taste got through to her, and instead, she held on.

His lips were demanding, unlocking a deep, quivering need inside her. Janna grasped his neck and kissed him back, forgetting that he was the boss and she was an employee whom he'd rescued from chickens only moments before. And she forgot that she was mad at men.

The only thing she knew was him, the firmness of his lips, the insistence of his mouth, the feel of his freshly shaven jaw, the clean scent of soap and shaving cream. When she'd kissed Michael, she had always felt he was in a hurry, mentally checking his watch to make sure he didn't waste too much time on it. Seth kissed as though he had all the time in the world and intended to do it right. His kiss was sweet enough to bring tears to her eyes and only served to add to the sense of belonging she'd experienced since her arrival at the ranch.

She was just convincing herself that she had the moral strength to stop when Seth ended the kiss. His brown eyes had darkened almost to black and his thick brows had drawn together into a line that spoke of puzzlement and perhaps disapproval. Janna gulped, trying to get her heart back into its proper place. "Why...why did you do that?"

The somberness cleared from his eyes, and he grinned. "So I wouldn't have to listen to you telling me that you can do whatever needs to be done one more time."

"Oh." What had she expected? A confession of wild, undying love for her?

Seth recovered much more quickly than she did, if recover could even be the word. He seemed totally unaffected by a kiss that had rocked her world.

"I think what you need is a lesson in chicken feeding. I keep forgetting what a tenderfoot you are. Though, heaven knows how it could slip my mind."

Janna watched his mouth form the words, but there seemed to be a terrible buzzing in her ears. She felt hot and cold by turns. "What? Oh, oh, yes." She shook her head. "And for a minute, I forgot what a take-charge kind of man *you* are. I don't have to go back in that coop right now, do I?" Her heart was hammering so hard against her ribs, she couldn't believe he didn't feel it.

His lips twitched into a wicked smile. "Certainly not. I can stand here and hold you just as long as you want me to."

"I don't want you to." She pushed against him.

He didn't budge. "It's fine to be afraid of something as long as you go right back and tackle it again."

"That sounds like something my dad would say."

"He must be a wise man."

"He's overbearing, like you."

"A man's gotta do what a man's gotta do," Seth intoned dramatically.

She resisted the urge to drop her head against his chest in surrender. "Oh, please don't get philosophical on me." Darn it, if he could be unaffected by that kiss, so could she. "All right, all right. Let me go, and you can show me the proper way to take eggs from chickens."

Seth released her immediately. "I knew you'd see it my way, but I don't think there are any eggs left to gather. You give new meaning to the phrase 'egg on your face.'"

Janna smirked at him, then looked down at the sticky mess that covered her—and him. "I never did get that evil hen's egg." She nodded toward the one that had started all the trouble, then examined the various wounds on her hands and feet. "I can guess why she's called Jackhammer."

"Gets you every time if you don't know how to deal with her. This time, watch your toes."

Sighing gratefully that their crazy moment of intimacy was past, Janna shoved her hair out of her face with a hand that shook ever so slightly. "Lead on, oh mighty rancher. Show me what to do."

He swung the gate open and ushered her back among the feathered fiends. "I'm glad you're so agreeable. As I said, I did the milking for you today, but tomorrow morning, I'll show you how."

Janna answered him with a sickly smile.

CHAPTER FIVE

OF COURSE, BREAKFAST WAS late. Seth had patiently shown Janna where the chicken feed was kept, how to scatter it around, and then how to distract Jackhammer so they could rob her nest. Janna was glad he didn't berate her for breaking all the other eggs.

Once they were finished in the henhouse, Janna and Seth both had to clean the egg off themselves. When she had changed into clean shorts and a shirt, Janna rushed back to work.

Although she wasn't quite sure how to use the fancy coffee maker, she managed to make coffee. Her plans for crepes had been spoiled by Jackhammer, so she started toasting bread, figuring any idiot could do that. She burned four pieces before she realized that the vintage toaster, in spite of what the setting said, didn't really know the meaning of "light." Since Seth loved gadgets and appliances so much, she couldn't figure out why he hadn't replaced the toaster. She decided it must have some antique value.

Of course, it was entirely possible that she wouldn't have burned the toast if she hadn't been leaning against the counter thinking about their kiss. Oh, how she hoped no one had seen them.

She finally stood over the toaster and watched as it attempted to char two more slices of bread, rescuing them just in time and slathering them with butter. With this method, she managed to toast a dozen pieces before the hands came in from the bunkhouse. The whole time, she thought of the disastrous breakfast Katharine Hepburn had made for Spencer Tracy in *Woman of the Year*. Thank goodness, she wasn't making waffles.

Feeling nicely domesticated, she poured out big glasses of orange juice and set them on the table. Steve and Gus asked after the filly, and Janna told them about their trip to Mrs. Berk's. They admitted they had been the ones to clean the kitchen, though she suspected they were embarrassed by doing what wasn't real "cowboy" work.

Seth came downstairs a few minutes later. Janna felt prickles of excitement at the thump of his dusty boots on the dining room floor. His dark hair was freshly combed and he was wearing a clean chambray shirt and jeans.

A cool breeze swept in with him, bringing her the scent of the outdoors and Seth's spicy after-shave. It reminded her of those terrified moments when she'd pressed her face into his back. The breeze almost dissipated the smell of scorched bread.

But not quite. Seth stopped near the table and sniffed the air. "What's for breakfast? Charcoal?"

His dark eyes held a teasing gleam, but Janna didn't see it for what it was; she thought he was having fun at her expense. She gave him an arch look. "Have you ever considered fixing the toaster?"

"Why? It works fine for Emmie." He grabbed a mug, poured himself some coffee and took a sip. To her disappointment, he grimaced.

"Whew. Next time, why don't you cut the amount of coffee grounds in half?" He went to the sink, poured out much of the contents and added hot water from the tap.

Through her teeth, she said, "All right, I will." Inwardly, she fumed over his criticism. Couldn't the man tell a polite little social lie and say the coffee was good?

Emmie shuffled in. She was dressed in a baggy pair of men's pajamas covered by a lime green chenille bathrobe. Janna thought she looked ghastly. Her face was haggard, and her skin had an odd cast to it, but that might have been the reflection from the bathrobe.

Emmie glanced around the kitchen and frowned. "Seth, quit picking on this girl. She works for me, remember? If you don't like the way she cooks, you can go into town to eat or cook for yourself." She seated herself at the table and carefully laid her injured wrist on its polished top, wincing at even that gentle contact. As if trying to ignore the pain, she picked up a piece of toast and bit into it. "Personally, I like charcoal. It's good for the teeth."

That made him laugh, and he came over to sit down beside her, asking how she felt. The Collins boys, along with Barker and José, had watched all this with interest and seemed to relax when Emmie arrived to defuse the situation. They poured themselves big bowls of cereal and dug in.

"How's your wrist?" Janna asked, carrying a dish of jam to the table and seating herself opposite Seth.

"Hurts."

"You're going to have it x-rayed today," Seth announced firmly, "If I have to hog-tie you and drag you there myself."

"Okay. Janna can take me in to Safford."

Seth choked on his coffee. He stared at her through watery eyes, then looked at Janna, before returning his gaze to Emmie. "Since when did you ever agree so readily to anything I wanted?"

"Since I had a reason to."

Janna laughed this time. Her eyes sparkled at Seth as she reached for a bowl and poured cereal into it.

He scowled at the two of them. "And what's your reason?"

"I need to look in on Sue Perritt, and besides, this thing hurts worse than I thought it would. At my age, I can't take a chance on having a broken bone. I may not be around long enough to watch it heal."

Having delivered that bit of shaky logic, Emmie finished her toast. As Janna ate, she thought with relief that this meal was much easier than the one they'd shared at Wally's Discount City, when she'd been trying to convince Seth to hire her. Now she just had to make sure he didn't regret doing it.

Seth and the boys were busy packing away their food, barely breathing between mouthfuls. She had a vague notion that breakfast cereals were pretty expensive, though, and weren't something she should serve every day. Let him laugh at her toast-making. Tomorrow she would make some Danish pastries that would knock Seth Brody's boots off. She sipped her juice and smiled at the thought.

"What's so funny?" he asked.

"Nothing," she said, manufacturing an innocent expression. "Absolutely nothing."

He wouldn't let it drop, of course. "Can you ride?"

She went very still, then touched the tip of her tongue to the corner of her mouth. "That depends on what you mean by ride."

The men snickered, then coughed into their napkins when Seth scowled at them. "I mean can you get yourself into the saddle, grab the reins and yell 'giddap'? Can you stay in the saddle and control the horse with your knees, voice and hands?"

Janna drew in a deep breath and widened her eyes. Exhaling slowly, she said, "No."

Emmie giggled, the boys grinned and Seth groaned. "I should have known. Well, you're not going to be much help during roundup, then."

"I thought I was only supposed to cook."

Seth bit into a piece of toast. "We'll need everyone's help."

"I can learn," she declared, her voice firm, even as she wondered when she had developed such a stubborn streak. He gave her a steady look, but the corner of his mouth twitched as if he was trying to control a laugh. "So I've heard."

The conversation changed to the day-to-day running of the ranch, but Janna was no longer listening.

Roundup! That sounded like fun. Janna envisioned something from an old Hollywood B movie. *The Three Mesquiters,* maybe, in which the spiffily dressed cowboys and cowgirls sat around the camp fire at night, eating beans and biscuits and then yodeling to the accompaniment of a guitar. After the camp fire was banked for the night, they would roll out their bedding, rest their heads on their saddles and go to sleep beneath the stars. It would be a new experience for her. She had never been camping before.

"How many days will we be gone?" she asked abruptly.

The others seemed surprised by her question, which obviously had no bearing on their conversation, but Seth answered, "Every day for a week."

A week! She liked the idea of camping, but a whole week without a bathroom? A week of cooking over a camp fire when she could barely cook at all? She could hardly stand to think about it, but since Seth was watching her carefully, she nodded and said, "Fine. Where do you keep the camping equipment?"

Emmie snickered and looked over at her partner. "Well, you've got to admit one thing, she's not afraid of a challenge."

"More guts than brains."

Janna was about to protest when Emmie spoke up. "Watch yourself, son. You're not so big that I can't turn you over my knee," the feisty older lady warned.

That image was so ridiculous that everyone burst out laughing. The ranch hands pushed back their chairs and headed outside, still chuckling.

Seth didn't follow them. Instead, he said, "I think you've got the wrong idea about this, Janna. We round up, brand and vaccinate the calves during the day, but come home at night. We don't sleep out under the stars."

Janna began clearing the table. As usual, pride got in her way. "I knew that."

"Sure you did." Seth stood and moved toward the door.

Emmie looked up in surprise. "Don't you want some more coffee? You usually have two cups."

He glanced at her, then at Janna. "No, thanks. I like my stomach lining just the way it is."

It was a struggle, but Janna managed to keep from sticking her tongue out at him.

Emmie watched this exchange with sharp eyes and said, thoughtfully, "Since you're going to be gone on roundup from dawn 'til dusk, and I can't help with the cooking, anyway, I think I'll go stay with Edith Collins 'til you're all finished. We're going to visit her today. I'll just pack a bag."

Seth settled his hat on his head. "I could leave Barker here. You wouldn't be alone."

"I need a vacation. Besides, I talked to Edith last night while you were out bouncing around the county seeing a chiropractor about Goldie's foal. Seems she's organizing a bridge tournament."

"You've got a sprained wrist."

Emmie gave him an arch look. "The day I can't play bridge, sprain or no sprain, is the day I'll hang up my spurs." With that confusing assurance, she returned her attention to her breakfast.

Grinning, Seth headed for the door. "Well, good luck."

"Thanks, I'll need it." She sat, sipping her coffee while Janna worked.

With her hands full of cereal bowls, Janna turned from the table and saw that Seth had stopped in the back hallway. He was gazing into her bedroom where she had left her bed unmade in her rush to get the eggs gathered.

Janna knew what he saw. She wasn't accustomed to picking up after herself, but that would change immediately. However, she couldn't change the way the bed looked. She was a restless sleeper—all over the bed at night, kicking off covers, then tangling herself in them. Her pillows invariably landed on the floor. Although she had been exhausted last night, her sleeping habits remained the same. It looked as if a dryer full of linens had exploded in the pretty little bedroom.

Seth must have felt her watching him because he turned, his boots grinding the worn linoleum, to look at her. Emotions shifted in his dark eyes—the same emotions she had seen when he had kissed her. She would have expected to see condemnation for her sloppy habits; instead, she saw a flicker of desire, but it was quickly extinguished. Whipping around, he shoved through the screen door, letting it slam behind him.

Janna released a slow breath and felt the tightness around her heart easing. Still, she was unaccountably disappointed that he hadn't said goodbye, or wished her a good day.

Emmie carried her cup to the sink. "I'll be ready to head for town as soon as I'm dressed. Can you come up in a bit to help me pack a bag?"

"Of course," Janna replied, barely noticing when the other woman left the kitchen. She was watching Seth pull on his gloves as he headed toward the barn. She set the stack of bowls she'd been holding by the sink, then gripped the sink's cool stainless steel edge. Seth walked with unstudied, virile grace, his long legs carrying him across the yard in swift strides. He stopped for a moment and petted the two collies that roamed the yard, scratching their ears and speaking to them. When he started off again, they followed at his boot heels.

Janna had to admit he was an attractive man. And until the roundup was over, the two of them would be alone in this house at night.

Janna looked down at her hands as they rested on the edge of the sink. Only three days ago she had been furious with men in general, and two in particular. Now she was watching Seth Brody's walk and thinking of spending nights in the same house with him. The abruptness of her change of heart disturbed her. How was she ever going to get through the next few weeks?

IN SPITE OF Emmie's assurances to the contrary, her wrist was broken. The break was clean, though, and the doctor said it would heal well if Emmie was careful. Janna and Emmie then looked in on Sue Perritt, who was sleeping, still groggy from her surgery.

Their last stop was at the home of Edith Collins, who turned out to be as talkative as her grandsons were quiet. By the time Janna had bid Emmie goodbye, with promises that everything would be fine, it was after noon, and she had to hurry back to the ranch. When she drove up to the house, she again experienced a sense of homecoming, as well as prickles of trepidation. She was truly on her own now. All her big words about proving herself were coming back to haunt her.

Once inside the house, she resolutely put away her purse and headed back to the kitchen. Evidence of the men's lunch was everywhere. They had made themselves sandwiches—if the amount of bread wrappers, smoked ham packages and condiment jars scattered about the counters was any indication. Discouraged, Janna looked at the mess for a minute, remembering the pride she'd felt at the kitchen's neatness just a few hours before. Then she set to work.

Being the one responsible for a kitchen put a whole new perspective on things. She was embarrassed by the way she'd always left messes for Fiona, her family's housekeeper, to clean up. Now she realized it wasn't much fun cleaning up after other people, even if she was getting paid for it. She was determined to be more considerate of Fiona once she returned home.

But she was home. The unbidden thought troubled her, and she pushed it aside, reminding herself that this job was only temporary.

After she had the kitchen cleaned up, Janna searched through Emmie's cookbooks and found a recipe for pepper steak that seemed fairly simple. Seth wouldn't need to teach her how to cook steaks, after all.

She was in charge of the house and Emmie's bedroom was the only room she'd seen upstairs, so Janna decided to do some exploring. She took along a feather duster as an excuse.

There were four bedrooms and two bathrooms upstairs. Emmie had the largest room, the one she'd shared with her husband since they'd bought the ranch in the late sixties. On the wall opposite the bed, there was an oil painting of a grizzled cowboy on horseback. Emmie had told her it was a portrait of her husband painted by a neighbor.

Janna paused for a moment to study the artist's technique, intrigued by the vitality that had been captured. He had young eyes in a lined face, and Janna felt as if he was on the verge of telling a funny story.

The strength of character in the old cowboy's face made her think of her father, who was long on strength and character, but short on sensitivity. With a pang, she thought of her mother and brothers, who she knew were probably worried about her. Her father would worry, too, but Ben Whitley was too stubborn to admit that Janna may have left because of something he did. If she went back now, or even called, he would try to rule her for the rest of her life. He called her stubborn. If that was true, she had learned from a master. She missed him, but she was determined that things would be different once she returned home. That decided, she squared her shoulders and went to explore the other rooms.

Seth's room was the last one at the end of the hall. It had windows that faced north and west, looking out over the apple orchard. His room was plainly furnished with a neatly made double bed, a tall mahogany dresser and an old-fashioned rocker with a deep, padded seat. Janna couldn't resist sitting in it.

The rocker was just the right height for her, and she started rocking as she pictured Brody women of the past rocking and singing to their babies in this chair, as they looked out on the ripening apples and listened to the sounds of ranch life.

The peaceful moment made her think of home and of the window seat in her bedroom where she and her mother often curled up for a chat. She had a pretty good idea what her mother would say about everything that had happened. Although she would have applauded Janna's need to be on her own, she would have chided Janna for running away. She would have been livid with Janna for not telling Seth the complete truth about herself. Guiltily, Janna shifted in the rocker, making it squeak softly. When could she have told him? There had hardly been one quiet moment since she'd arrived. And what would he think if she told him? Probably that she was a spoiled rich girl.

With a sigh, she looked around the room, pushed her toe against the floor to set the chair in motion and resumed her dreaming.

It occurred to her that Seth would be the last Brody to rock in this chair. He had been adamant when he said he wouldn't marry, that life on Fawn Creek was too rough for a woman. And yet, generations of Brody women had done it. Why was he so opposed to having a wife? Emmie had told her he was an only child. Who would inherit the ranch after him? No doubt, it would pass into other hands. She wondered why he would let that happen when he had worked so hard to get the ranch back in the family.

Janna touched her lips. He had kissed her that morning knowing he was safe—*she* was mad at men, and *he* didn't intend to get involved with anyone. That kiss hadn't meant anything to him and shouldn't to her. So why did it?

Seth was a disturbing man, so sure of himself, yet she saw flashes of vulnerability in his eyes that made her wonder how determined he really was to spend the rest of his life alone.

She stood and wandered around the room, stopping beside the bed to run her hand over the carved mahogany headboard, then across the nubbly weave of the midnight blue spread.

Sitting on the side of the bed, she bounced lightly, testing the mattress. From the looks of things, Seth didn't need a housekeeper, just a cook. He picked up after himself.

Or did he? Janna recalled that her brothers' idea of picking up after themselves consisted of kicking their belongings under the bed. Twisting around, she lay on her stomach across the bed and scooted to the edge. She pulled up the bedskirt and leaned over until her long, thick hair swept the floor.

Nope, no shoes, clothing, or discarded sports equipment. Not even so much as a dustball. Seth really was as neat as he appeared to be.

So absorbed was she in her thoughts, that she didn't know she was being watched until a pair of boots appeared at the edge of her vision. She turned her head. No, those definitely hadn't been there a few minutes ago. She reached out a cautious hand. Yep, they were real, all right. Sweeping her hair out of the way, she turned her head and let her gaze travel up long, dusty jeans, over a torn chambray shirt, to Seth Brody's puzzled face.

Janna smiled brightly. "I'll bet you're wondering what I'm doing down here, aren't you?"

"Yeah, and I can't wait to hear your explanation."

Flushing as bright as a Christmas tree bulb, she got herself to her feet. Straightening her shirt with great dignity, she said, "I was checking for dust."

Seth folded his arms over his chest and nodded sagely. "I see."

Although she felt utterly foolish and knew her best course of action would be to keep her mouth shut, she blurted out, "You know how dust kind of collects in places?"

"Oh, yeah. It's always been one of my big worries."

"Has it?" Her voice squeaked, and she cleared her throat. Her fingers came up to play with her gold chain. Why did she get herself into these messes? "That's too bad." She scuffed her shoe and clapped her palms together. "Sooo, I'll just keep on with my work here."

Seth came closer with an I've-got-you-now smile. "Did you find any?"

Janna stepped back and snatched up the feather duster. Nonchalantly, she brushed the ostrich feathers against her hand. "Any what?"

"Dust."

"No. I'm happy to say it's clean under your bed."

"That sure takes a load off my mind."

"I'll . . . I'll just finish the dusting. . . ." With color high on her cheeks, she wielded the feather duster over the top of the immaculate dresser, her zealousness causing her to sneeze.

Still chuckling, Seth strode across the room and gave her a sardonic glance. "Bless you. I can tell you're hard at work so I won't disturb you." As he spoke, he started removing his shirt, which was ripped down the front.

Not disturb her! He had to be kidding. The sight of his chest and sinewy arms sent her temperature soaring. She couldn't seem to stop watching him while he removed a clean shirt from the closet, shrugged into it and began snapping it up. When he started to unbutton his jeans to tuck the shirttail inside, her mind finally resumed functioning and she moved toward the door.

"I'll, um, I'll go finish with my—" she took a deep breath "—my whatever."

Grinning at her discomfort, he followed her out into the hall and handed her his torn shirt. "This thing's so old, there's no point mending it."

Janna blinked at him. She was expected to mend, too? She couldn't even thread a needle. "Oh, I see."

"Emmie uses them for rags when they can't be fixed anymore." With that, he turned and went down the stairs, leaving her reeling from his nearness and from the unique combination of musk and sweat rising from the torn shirt.

She leaned weakly against the wall and tried to get her breath back. It served her right for daydreaming on the job when she should have been working. Determined not to be caught like that again, she fled to the kitchen and tried to calm herself by rereading the pepper steak recipe.

If she followed the directions exactly, she was convinced she couldn't go wrong. The steak was easy to come by, since there was a freezer full of it, but the peppercorns eluded her. She couldn't imagine that in a kitchen as well stocked as Emmie's there would be no peppercorns. Eventually, she found some in an unlabelled bottle tucked into the back corner of a cabinet. She put it with the other ingredients, then turned to baking.

This was something she could do well. She made pastries for breakfast the next morning and baked chocolate chip cookies. She was just pulling the last cookie sheet from the oven when Steve and Gus came in. The hungry looks on their faces reminded her of cartoon characters, who floated freely above the earth when smelling something delicious. She experienced a twisting pang of homesickness for her brothers, Jeff and Jeremy. "Hi, guys," she greeted them.

"Smells good in here," Steve commented, his eyes glued to the cooling cookies.

"Awesome," Gus agreed.

Taking pity on them, Janna said, "Wash your hands, and I'll give you some." As they rushed off to do as she bid, an idea occurred to her. When they returned, she not only had a plate of cookies ready for them, but also tall glasses of cold milk. "Guys, I want you to look on this as a bribe."

They glanced at each other uneasily, then at the snack. "A bribe?" Gus asked.

She pulled out a chair and sat down opposite them, looking eagerly into their faces. "Yes. I need to learn how to ride. And I think you guys can teach me. As payment, I'll bake you all the cookies you want."

The boys brightened and took several cookies apiece. "All we have to do is teach you to ride?"

"That's right." She grinned smugly, thinking of the surprised look on Seth's face when she rode a horse all by herself.

Again, the boys exchanged glances, as if communicating silently. "I suppose we could do that."

"Good." In celebration, Janna took a couple of cookies for herself. "When can we start?" She bit into the rich chocolate and pecan confection, savoring the taste as much as she savored the thought of Seth's surprise.

"Tomorrow morning after we finish the chores Seth gave us," Steve announced, reaching for another handful of cookies.

WHEN THE MEN CAME IN for dinner that night, Janna was ready for them. Before starting the pepper steak, she had read the recipe over five times. She had also baked potatoes, cooked some of Emmie's frozen green beans and whipped up a huge pan of biscuits.

Standing by the table, she surveyed the dinner a little uncertainly. The potatoes didn't look quite like the ones Fiona made. Janna's were shrunken inside their skins. And the beans were a little limp—okay, more than a little. Janna chewed on her bottom lip, wondering if it would help to drown them in butter. But she decided against it. Why add even more cholesterol to this meal?

The biscuits were perfect, though, and the steak looked good. The peppercorns dotted the crispy outside, and the inside seemed tender. At least it had the dozen or so times she'd cut into it to check. Satisfied at last, she went to the back door and rang the bell that Emmie had said was the signal that dinner was ready.

Within a few minutes, the men were crowded around the table—except for Seth, who was checking on Goldie and Silver.

The men handed around the food and dug in. Janna sat on the edge of her chair, waiting for their verdict.

Seeing the anxiety on her face, José saluted her with his knife, cut off a piece of steak and popped it into his mouth. Barker, Gus and Steve did the same.

Four jaws began to move in unison. Then four jaws stopped, and four hands grabbed for glasses of iced tea.

"What's wrong?" she asked. "Did I use too much pepper?"

"No, *señorita*," José answered in a faintly strangled voice. "I wouldn't say that." He gave the other men a warning look and added, "It's fine. Just fine." He lifted a biscuit and slathered it with butter. "And how about these biscuits, huh, *amigos?* This lady can really make biscuits."

Puzzled, Janna picked up her steak knife just as Seth came in.

"What's wrong?" he asked, looking from one employee to the next. The men were all heartily munching on biscuits, avoiding the meat as if it was infected with plague germs.

"I don't know," Janna admitted, cutting into her own piece of the steak.

Seth leaned across the table and plucked the fork from her fingers. He popped it into his mouth and chewed. A strange expression passed over his face, and he spoke around the food in his mouth. "What's this supposed to be?"

"Pepper steak." She commandeered the fork from his place setting, cut herself another piece of meat and bit into it.

Seth swallowed with difficulty. "This isn't pepper steak. What we have here is juniper berry steak."

By now Janna was tasting the strange piney flavor herself. It wasn't bad exactly, but it wasn't very good, either. She chewed and swallowed, managing not to shudder as it slid down her throat. "Junipers are those evergreen bushes out back, aren't they?"

"That's right." Seth went to the refrigerator and grabbed a big bottle of ketchup. "Did you go out and pick some berries?"

"Of course not," she answered, huffily. "I found what I thought was pepper in the cabinet."

With a sigh, Seth passed the ketchup around. "And I suppose you didn't think the stuff smelled funny when it was cooking."

Her tone grew frosty. "No." The truth was, she didn't know what it should have smelled like because she'd never cooked it before. He didn't have to embarrass her in front of everybody. Head high, she took the remaining meat to the sink, flicked off the dried berries and returned the platter to the table. "Maybe if you drown it in ketchup, you won't be able to tell."

José gave her another salute. Ignoring the mocking slant to Seth's mouth, Janna smiled gratefully at the older man. She knew the meal wasn't a complete disaster. Everything else was edible, especially the biscuits. Defiantly, she passed a plateful of them to Seth, thinking, *Just you wait, Seth Brody. I'll prove myself yet.* The returning challenge in his dark eyes seemed to say, *I'll wait a long time.*

The next morning, Janna met the Collins boys at the corral. Seth and the other men had gone to one of the pastures to mend fences, leaving Steve and Gus to clean the corral and barn. They had rushed through their chores while Janna had cleaned up the kitchen and made another batch of cookies, peanut butter this time. She carried them outside in a paper bag. If she was going to bribe, she was going to bribe promptly. "Okay, what do I need to know first?" she asked, handing Steve the bag of cookies.

"How to saddle," Gus answered, leading a big chestnut stallion from the barn. Spying the paper bag that his brother was plundering, he made a short detour. With his mouth full of peanut butter cookie, he said, "At least, saddling is what Seth taught us first. This is Salsa. He was the horse Seth taught us on."

Seeing the stallion, Janna's mouth went dry. He was huge, much bigger than Goldie! His back was level with Janna's head. She estimated that by the time she was in the saddle, she would be eight or nine feet off the ground. Swallowing hard, she watched as Steve and Gus showed her how to put the bridle in Salsa's mouth. They simply grasped his nose and pulled his mouth open, exposing teeth that were as long as Janna's thumb. He accepted the bridle easily from them, but when Janna tried, the horse rolled two big brown eyes, as if asking who she was kidding. He refused to open his mouth, simply baring his clenched teeth at her and pulling his head away.

Although she tried not to show how frustrated she was, it obviously showed, because Steve took the bridle from her and put it on himself. "Maybe you'll do better with the saddle," he reassured her. "This kind of thing just takes practice."

Janna nodded, telling herself she wasn't nervous. Gus held Salsa's head while Steve showed her what to do with the blanket and saddle. Janna grabbed the saddle horn in one hand and the cantle in the other. Lifting, she staggered beneath the weight of the gear, and it was only with a mighty heave that she managed to toss it onto Salsa's back, bumping up against his flank as she did so. The horse sidestepped nervously, but Gus soothed him.

Regaining her balance, Janna looked up—and sighed.

"Uh, Janna..."

"I know. I know. I got it on backward." Reaching up, she pulled the saddle off the horse, turned it around and tried again. This time, she got it right, and Steve continued the lesson by showing her how to tighten the cinches. "Always mount from the left, otherwise, you might get thrown or stepped on." Janna glanced down at Salsa's hooves. Pulverized was more like it. Nodding at Steve's list of instructions, she reached up, trying to fit her sneakered left foot into the high stirrup. When she managed that, her right foot dangled an inch or so above the ground. Awkwardly she bounced, trying to lift herself up.

Before Steve could lower the stirrups or give her a boost, Salsa decided he was tired of the tenderfoot, so he tossed his head, jerking the reins from Gus's loose hold, and loped away.

"Wait!" Janna cried, hopping along on one foot. Her left foot slipped forward to the ankle, catching in the stirrup. "Whoa!" But Salsa only moved faster. Fearful that if she let go, she would be dragged, Janna continued hopping like a one-legged frog.

Steve and Gus ran beside her, shouting frantically as they tried to stop the horse, but when they came close to Salsa, he shied the other way. If they approached him from the front, he backed and turned, taking Janna with him.

Janna's fingers were gripping the saddle horn so tightly they were white. Her head whipped around, as she hollered for help.

At last, she realized that if she let her right foot drag, it might slow him down a bit. It did. When she stopped hopping, the huge horse reared onto his hind legs and tossed her into the dust.

CHAPTER SIX

STUNNED, JANNA LAY on the ground, trying to get her breath back. She blinked against the sun's glare, then tried to focus. Above her were six heads. She closed her eyes and looked again. The six heads merged into three, one of which was Seth's. He pushed the two boys aside and reached for her.

Running his hands over her, he checked for broken bones, then lifted her to a sitting position. "Janna, are you all right?"

She nodded, gasped and burped.

"I guess you are," he responded with a soft chuckle. Supporting her with one hand, he looked up at the boys. "Catch that damned horse and turn him out into the pasture. He's the wrong horse for her to learn on."

"Why?" Steve asked, as Gus grabbed Salsa's reins.

"Because he's a misogynist."

"Huh?"

"A woman hater. For some reason, he can't stand women."

Janna sucked air into her lungs. "And you've got a chicken that hates toes. What are you running? A ranch for misfits?"

"Tut-tut, Miss Whitley," Seth chided her as the boys took care of the horse. "Sounds to me like you're the misfit around here. I've known you less than three days, and I've had to drag you out of several scrapes already. I should think you'd be more grateful."

"I will be as soon as I find out if I can still walk." She hated admitting that, but he'd find out for himself if he made her stand too soon and she melted back into the dust like the Wicked Witch of the West. Janna desperately wanted to rub the muscles on the insides of her thighs, but not with Seth watching. Taking a deep breath, she steeled herself and allowed him to help her to her feet. She stumbled, but he caught her, wrapping an arm around her waist to steady her until she felt strong enough to hold herself upright.

"I've got to tell you, Janna, I don't think you've got a future doing bird imitations. Your landings need work."

She gave him a sour look. "Very funny. I thought you were mending fences."

Seth was busy running his hands over her head, apparently checking for lumps. "Needed more supplies. Why don't you sit down for a minute while I go saddle Hildy? She's a gentle mare."

"You mean I have to get back on?" Janna tried to control the quiver in her voice, but it slipped through.

"Of course. How else will you learn?"

"I don't suppose you have a video I could watch, do you?"

His eyes laughed at her as he led her to a bench beside the barn door and set her gently down. "I thought you were the woman who could do anything. Look how you took on those chickens this morning. You gathered the eggs without a problem."

"Yeah, well, I don't have to ride the darned chickens."

When he didn't answer, she looked up. Seth was watching her, his strong features made boyishly appealing by his knowing grin. His hat was pushed to the back of his head, and he had his hands tucked into the rear pockets of his jeans as he stood there with challenge in his eyes. She had to admit that he'd been remarkably patient with her. Having her around certainly wasn't making his job any easier. "Don't you have something to do that's more important?"

"Yeah, about a hundred somethings, but you won't learn unless somebody teaches you, and since I'm the boss, it looks like I'm elected."

"Just what I need," she muttered, "a conscientious boss. Oh, all right." She flapped her hand at him. "Go get the horse. I'll try again."

His expression told her he approved. "Good girl. Do you have any jeans and boots?"

"Jeans."

"Go put them on and look in Emmie's closet for a pair of boots. You might find some that'll fit. If you'd had boots on, the heel would have helped you mount Salsa, and you wouldn't have done that one-legged bunny hop around the corral."

She didn't want to move, but she limped over to the house anyway. She changed into jeans and dragged herself upstairs to find a pair of boots. They were too tight, but she figured that didn't matter because she wasn't going to do much walking in them.

When she got back to the corral, Seth was sending the Collins boys off with an extra roll of wire and more staples for the hands who were mending fences. He went into the barn and brought out Hildy, leading her over to where Janna sat. Hildy was brown, with four black feet and a black mane. She lifted gentle brown eyes to look at Janna, who was watching her warily.

"Good," Seth commented softly. "Show her you're at least her equal. Come here."

Reluctantly, Janna did as he said, moving to stand beside him. Hildy was quiet, unlike Salsa, who had twitched and shied whenever she came near.

"Blow in her face," Seth commanded.

"Blow?"

"I know it sounds crazy, but she needs to get used to you." Janna did as he said, blowing gently into the mare's nose. Hildy whinnied softly, then nudged her.

"She likes you," Seth said.

"Yeah, but do I like her?"

"Only one way to find out." He handed Janna the bridle. "Push up on her nose with the heel of your hand. She'll accept the bit automatically."

To Janna's surprise, he was right, and her confidence grew as he led her through each step of bridling and saddling.

"Be firm, but not rough," Seth told her. "Riding is an agreement between a strong partner and a smart partner—you're supposed to be the smart one. The boss. You have to know what you want, and you have to tell her.''

"Do I whisper it in her ear?'' Even though she was quite proud of her saddling job, she was still shaky from having been thrown and didn't want a repeat performance.

"No, you use body language. Yours and hers.'' Seth checked the tightness of the cinch, lowered the stirrup for her and stood back. "Come on. I'll help you into the saddle.''

With more than a little reluctance, Janna put her foot in the cradle he'd made of his hands, then boosted herself up and into the saddle.

Pleased that she had made it this far, but nervous at being on the horse's back, Janna sat stiffly, waiting for Seth's next instructions. They weren't long in coming. She jumped when he put his hands on her, one on her stomach, which quivered at his touch, and one on the small of her back. "Relax,'' he ordered.

Her jaw dropped halfway to her top button. He had to be kidding! With his hands searing right through the denim of her jeans, she was doing well just to keep breathing. She tried to shift away, but his grip only tightened.

"Don't fidget. Move forward in the saddle a little.'' That she could do, scooting up until he said, "Okay. Here's your center of gravity. You'll have the best balance if you remember exactly how this feels.''

How could she ever forget? Wildly, she tried to think of something to say, but her tongue was stuck to the roof of her mouth.

"Janna, do you understand what I'm saying?"

"Sure," she croaked.

"Don't be nervous. Hildy's not going to hurt you."

"It's not Hildy I'm worried about," she blurted.

His head came up then, and his hands flexed, as if he wanted to move them higher. He looked into her eyes, then down at her lips, telling Janna he was thinking the same thing she was, although probably without the self-condemnation she was experiencing.

She wanted to tumble off Hildy's back, straight into his arms, knowing that he would catch her, keep her safe. She also knew that it was perfectly ridiculous to be feeling this tug of sexual awareness—for two reasons. First, he was her boss, for goodness' sake. And second, she was still mad at men. Wasn't she?

Yet, here was Seth holding her firmly on the mare's back, his face full of hunger. But he didn't want the same things she wanted. Not that she could have said what it was she *did* want at this particular moment. Then Hildy shied sideways, breaking the spell that Janna and Seth seemed to be under.

Seth soothed the mare and resumed his instructions, showing Janna how to sit and how to hold the reins with the ends trailing loosely over her little fingers. "Pretend you're holding two baby birds and don't want to crush them," he told her, and she nodded.

Keeping his hand on the bridle, he began leading Hildy around, all the while giving instructions. "Use your peripheral vision. Breathe from your diaphragm. Keep your balance. Cutting horse riders can't stay in the saddle unless they're balanced.''

"I'm not a cutting horse rider,'' she pointed out grimly, watching the ground as it passed between Hildy's upright ears. "I'm not even a rider, yet. Let go of the bridle now.''

"Don't say it,'' he warned.

"What?''

"That you can do it.''

She flicked him a glance. "Well, I *can.*''

On a soft laugh, he stepped back. "Go ahead. Show me your stuff.''

Once she did as he said and relaxed in the saddle, riding was easier than she'd expected it to be. He called out instructions, correcting her posture or her seat. After an hour, he pronounced that it was time to dismount. Disappointed, because she was quite pleased with her progress, she nodded. He held the horse and told Janna how to dismount.

Cockily sure of herself, Janna threw her right leg over the saddle, preparing to kick free of the left stirrup and jump down. Her plan went awry when Seth reached up to help. Startled by the feel of his hands on her waist, she lost her balance.

Hildy sidestepped, causing Janna to topple backward into Seth's arms and pitching them both into the dirt. They landed in a tangle of arms and legs, with Janna's bottom square in the middle of Seth's belt buckle.

"Janna, get off,'' he grunted. "I can't breathe.''

"As if I can," she gasped, but managed to roll to the side.

Hildy, apparently disdainful of the antics of the two-legged creatures, trotted sedately over to the horse trough made from an old iron bathtub and began drinking.

After a few moments, Seth propped himself on an elbow and looked at Janna. His hat was gone, having been knocked off by the impact of their fall. His dark hair was flecked with dust and bits of straw, as was one cheek. He drew in a breath. "I'd say that your dismounting technique needs a little work. Unless you plan to continue getting off a horse that way."

Air finally found its way into Janna's lungs as she stared up at the sun. "I'll le...let you know. Actually, I'm getting u...used to looking at the world from this angle. Gives th...things a whole new perspective."

"Janna, having you around gives *life* a whole new perspective."

She turned her head and grinned at him. "Are you saying your life was boring before I came?"

"At least I knew what to expect from one day to the next."

"Well, who wants a life like that? It'll make you old before your time."

"Hey, I just want the chance to *get* old."

The sun was suddenly blocked as Seth leaned over her. The laughter had gone from his eyes, leaving them dark and mysterious.

"Janna, you're a constant puzzle to me."

"I am?"

"Yes. You're well educated, but don't seem to have a real career, which is a bit unusual for a woman nowadays."

Janna listened cautiously, wondering if she should tell him that her father was wealthy so she didn't have to work unless she wanted to. She'd only worked at the art gallery because she had loved it.

"And you've got family, but as far as I can tell, they don't know where you are, and you don't want them to know." He touched the auburn curls around her face. "Don't you think that's a little cruel?"

Not as cruel as the way he was making her feel. She needed to tell him the truth about herself—now!

"Seth, I—"

"Be quiet. You talk too much."

Then he kissed her, slowly and deliberately as if he had been giving it a great deal of thought and had decided this was the perfect time to do it.

And it was. His last kiss had been a tease. This was pure tenderness, first brushing against her lips from side to side, then taking ownership of them. He demanded more—and she gave it, acquiescing with tiny soft sounds from the back of her throat. She forgot what she'd been ready to tell him.

Seth slid his arms around her, lifting her out of the dust, one kiss following another until all she could do was willingly give him what he asked for.

She felt as if she was burning up, and it had nothing to do with the summer sun. It was Seth, indelibly imprinting himself on her feelings, her mind.

At last, the voice of sanity made itself heard. They were lying in the dusty corral, she thought in a haze. Anyone could come along and see them. Janna drew away. "Seth, we . . . we shouldn't be doing this here."

Denied her lips, he kissed the tiny cleft in her chin, sending delicious tremors shimmying through her. Then he buried his face in her hair. "Sweetheart," he murmured, "We shouldn't be doing this at all." He pulled air into his lungs, held it for a few seconds, then exhaled slowly.

He looked down at her then, his expression as unreadable as she'd ever seen it. "Janna, this isn't the life for you. Why don't you admit it?"

Stunned, she stared at the mouth that only moments ago had been kissing her breathless. "What?"

"You should go home. Your problems with your family can be worked out. I'll give you a month's salary in lieu of notice. Why don't you let me buy you a plane ticket home? I'll even drive you to the airport in Phoenix or Tucson, whichever one you want."

"Whichever one I..." She was still in his arms, but she felt as if the Grand Canyon had suddenly opened up between them. "No!" She jerked away from him and somehow managed to get to her feet. "I'm staying. I'm needed here." She was not going to run from another unhappy situation with a man. "There's nothing wrong with my work."

"That's not what I meant." He surged to his feet, slapped the dust from his hat and crammed it onto his head. "It's not your work."

"What is it, then?" She faced him, hands on hips. To her fury, tears stood in her eyes. "Are you attracted to me? Let me tell you something, mister. You kissed me. I kissed you back. Big deal. That doesn't mean anything." She took a deep breath, knowing she should be struck down for lying. "As long as it doesn't happen again, there's no harm done."

Another type of woman might have wondered why her father thought he had to run her life, or why her fiancé had turned to another woman, especially now that a third man was trying to send her away. Janna knew it wasn't her, though. This was Seth's problem, and it had something to do with his belief that she wasn't right for life on a ranch.

"Damn it, Janna, there's no guarantee that it won't happen again. It's not fair to you."

Clinging to the remains of her shattered dignity, Janna walked toward Hildy with a straight back. Once she caught the horse, she began loosening the cinch holding the saddle in place. "I don't need guarantees if you'll just keep your hands to yourself."

"I'll do that, Janna. I'll damned well do that." Seth stalked to his own horse, Mexico, who had spent the past hour patiently tied to the fence. "But we'll have another lesson tomorrow," he called as he swung into the saddle and spurred Mexico to a run.

Janna slumped against Hildy's neck and squeezed her eyes shut. A lesson in what?

THE REMAINDER of the week went better than she had expected, although she and Seth were cool and stand-offish with each other.

Janna's confidence in her cooking ability grew with each successful meal. The ones that weren't success-ful were fed to the chickens or the dogs, depending on which group was more likely to accept her offerings. She even managed to milk the cow, getting nearly a quart of liquid before her arms were exhausted and José had to take over. She learned to like milking, though. It was one of the few jobs she could do sit-ting down.

Her abilities as a housekeeper were still question-able. She accidentally left her purple T-shirt in the washer when she laundered Seth's underwear and turned his shorts a lovely shade of lavender. Knowing this wouldn't meet with his approval, she put in a frantic call to Emmie who laughed for a long time be-fore telling her how to bleach the unwanted color out. If Seth had noticed that his shorts had a strong chlo-rine smell, he hadn't said anything.

He continued their daily riding lessons, and al-though Janna no longer landed in the dirt, she was stiff and sore after each session. Part of this was due to her determination to ride as well as possible so he couldn't criticize her. She wasn't going to give him another opportunity to send her away.

She was coming to love life on the ranch. The work that needed to be done was hard, but straightforward and uncomplicated. Her job in California seemed like a distant dream now. She couldn't imagine what she had found appealing about selling overpriced—and sometimes just plain ugly—artwork to aimless and shallow people who were trying to figure out what they wanted from their lives.

Not so at the Diamond B Ranch. Everybody knew what they wanted—to please Seth. Gus and Steve worshiped him. José and Barker treated him with respect, and he returned the favor. He himself loved the ranch and the hard work that went along with it.

To Janna he was courteous, but distant. He kept his thoughts as private as she did, but she often caught him looking at her with the same intensity he'd shown when he'd kissed her. It both scared and exhilarated her, making her wonder what would happen if she made the first move toward him. She didn't do it, though, because she knew there would be consequences she couldn't handle.

Late at night, she could hear the faint creak of the floorboards as he wandered about, getting ready for bed. She imagined him in that big, high bed, in the room that overlooked the orchard. More than once, she relived their last kiss, or dreamed of being in that bed with him and could barely face him in the morning. If the other ranch hands sensed the tension in her, she hoped they put it down to her nervousness about the frequent mistakes she made.

In spite of her conflict over Seth, Janna was content. After dinner each night, everyone went their separate ways. José and Seth were teaching Steve and Gus how to rope, so the four of them often spent their evenings at the corral. The two boys had already graduated from roping fence posts to roping yearling calves. Barker had a girlfriend nearby who he visited in the evenings unless Seth had more work for him.

That left Janna to her own devices, which were few. Since the ranch was in a canyon, television reception was poor and the collection of country and western records that went with the stereo didn't really appeal to her. She had read her way through Emmie's collection of magazines, quietly disposing of the one that featured her and her mother. She wasn't the type to wile away time sitting on the porch swing, so she had begun working in the rose garden that took up most of the front yard.

Seth found her there one evening just before sundown, digging a trench to add rose food to the roots of a neglected Sterling Silver.

"Be sure to watch out for rattlers," he warned, leaning against the fence.

Alarmed, she jumped back as if she'd just been struck by one of the poisonous snakes. She glared at him. "Why can't you just tip your hat and say good evening?"

Mockingly, he did so. "Good evening, Miss Whitley. Watch out for rattlers."

She rolled her eyes at his theatrics. "Rattlers?"

"This is the time of evening they like to come out."

"To attack unsuspecting city slickers, no doubt," she said, glancing around.

He came through the gate and crouched beside her, balancing easily on the balls of his feet. He rested his forearms on his knees. "Don't worry, they usually give some warning before they strike."

"Oh, that makes me feel a whole lot better."

He looked down at her sandaled feet and grunted. "Maybe you should wear your boots to do this."

She laughed up at him. "Oh, that would look great with these shorts."

"Who'll see you? This isn't Hollywood. Besides, I thought you'd learned your lesson about wearing sandals out here."

Janna's head popped up, and she peered nervously through the gathering darkness toward the henhouse. "Aren't the hens roosting?"

"Yes, but Jackhammer's been known to sneak out and attack the unwary."

"That chicken has a thoroughly nasty disposition."

"Not if you know how to handle her." When she started to speak, Seth held up his hand. "I know, I know, you'll learn."

Satisfied that he was beginning to understand her determination, she went back to work and changed the subject. "Did Emmie plant these bushes?"

"No. That big white one was planted by my great-grandmother. She brought it from Texas in the back of a wagon. My grandmother carried on the tradition and planted all the others."

Janna pushed hair out of her eyes with the back of a dirty hand. "What about your mother?"

He snorted. "There weren't many traditions she carried on around here, including living here." Without another word, he stood and walked into the house, closing the glass-paned door firmly behind him.

Janna dusted earth from her hands. Did he mean that his mother hadn't liked it here?

Janna looked at the light spilling through the lace curtains at the front windows and felt the peace of the ranch steal over her.

Had his mother abandoned her family? Janna recalled what he'd said when they'd been lying in the corral dirt. Seth had wondered why she wouldn't call her family, why she had run away. She'd told him very little about her situation, and none of the truly important facts—like her father's wealth and his desire to run her life.

She needed to tell him. She needed to talk to him right now and tell him—as she had meant to days ago, just before he kissed her. But she remained where she was, slowly adding rose food to the roots of a hybrid tea. If she told him now, would his eyes hold the same censure for her that his voice had held for his mother?

CHAPTER SEVEN

ONE MORNING, when she had been at the Diamond B Ranch for a week, she went into Safford with a list of things Seth needed before the start of roundup. He'd also given her a week's pay and told her that the Fawn Creek community was having their annual barbecue the night before the Diamond B employees left on roundup. Seth had casually mentioned that she was invited, too. In honor of the occasion, Janna was going to buy a dress. She had one with her, but the pumpkin-colored raw silk sheath was far too fancy and sophisticated for a barbecue.

Of course, she could have paid with a credit card, or even used it to get a cash advance, but she was enjoying her independence and didn't want to take a chance that her father would find her.

In Safford, she visited a now alert and much improved Sue Perritt, who said she'd be released in a couple of days and would stay with Emmie at Edith Collins's house. She asked about life on the ranch and laughed so hard over Janna's mishaps that she had to hold her stitches.

At a little shop in town, Janna bought a peach-colored cotton dress made in the Mexican peasant style and big hoop earrings to go with it. Next, she got the things Seth had asked her for, then stopped to see Emmie and Edith Collins. The two ladies invited her in for lunch.

Afterward, Edith went to see a neighbor and left Janna alone with Emmie. Janna suspected this had been done by design when Emmie regarded her with a knowing smile and asked, "Well, how does the Beverly Hills debutante like living with the devil in blue jeans?"

Janna smiled and crimped the hem of her pleated yellow shorts between her fingers. "It's ... devilish, I guess." She repeated the stories she had told Sue and added, "He's really been very patient, considering I'm not the person he wanted. I didn't know how to do much of anything and trouble just seems to follow me."

Emmie cocked her head to one side, exactly like a bright-eyed bird, and said, "Patience is one thing he has in abundance. It took him twenty-five years to get back where he wanted to be, but he never gave up. He knew he'd make it."

Janna frowned. "Where he wanted to be?"

"At the ranch. He grew up in Phoenix, you know."

"Yes, he told me that on my first day. He was very matter-of-fact about it. He also said something once about his mother not wanting to live on the Diamond B."

Even though she felt a little guilty about prying into Seth's private life, she was wildly curious and wanted to know more about him and his family. She justified it by reminding herself that *she* was part of his life now.

"That's right. She couldn't stand it there. It was too isolated. You see, his mother, Miriam, met Lowell Brody in Phoenix and after they were married, moved to the ranch with him. Her family was wealthy. Her dad owned a big plastics manufacturing plant. I guess she thought life would carry on pretty much as it always had." Emmie smiled ruefully. "The poor girl had a rude awakening. My husband and I were working on a ranch nearby and saw what was happening."

"What?" Janna was already sitting on the edge of her chair, but she leaned forward even more.

Emmie propped her chin on her good wrist and thought for a minute. "Miriam expected it to be like a dude ranch, I think. You know, plenty of servants and drinks served at five o'clock by a white-jacketed waiter. Lowell did hire someone to help out in the house, though he couldn't really afford it. Miriam still had to do a lot of the work herself, especially after Seth was born. She was reasonably satisfied as long as she could get out, see friends, or visit her parents in Phoenix once a month or so. To give her credit, she didn't complain, at first."

"But that didn't last long?"

"No. The winter of 1967 we had the biggest snow I've ever seen in this area. It was five feet deep on the ground and the drifts were even higher. No one could get to their barns for days, and couldn't get into town for weeks. Miriam just snapped. She told Lowell it was her or the ranch. He brought Seth over to our house

so they could talk without scaring the boy to death—
he was only seven, after all.''

"But Seth's father couldn't change her mind?"

"No. In fact, by the time he got back from our
place, she'd packed her and Seth's things and was
loading them in her car." Emmie's face was sad. "She
wouldn't even relent enough to let him keep the ranch
with someone else running it. I suppose she was afraid
that if he kept even partial ownership he'd be tempted
to come back. He sold it to us, got a job at his father-
in-law's company and never returned.''

"But the ranch had been in the family for three
generations. How could he stand to sell it?"

"Miriam was more important. That's the way the
Brody men are, Janna. When they love someone, they
hang on to her. Lowell loved Miriam more than he
loved the ranch.''

"How did Seth take the news?"

"He fought like a hellcat.''

Janna laughed.

"I'm serious. When they were ready to leave, he
grabbed the door frame and wouldn't let go. When
they pried his hands off, he grabbed the porch railing, wrapped his arms and legs around it and screamed
bloody murder. When they got him away from that
and dragged him down the sidewalk, he grabbed the
gate post so hard I thought we'd have to dig it up and
send it along with him. They finally got him loose, but
he ended up with splinters all over both hands. We
could hear the poor little guy yelling all the way down

the hill. Lowell told me later that he cried all the way to Phoenix. Four and a half hours.''

Janna sat back, limp, imagining Seth as a terrified little boy, leaving the home he loved. "He came back, though."

"Yes. He didn't thrive in Phoenix. Oh, he went to school, played Little League, made friends and everything, but Lowell said he grieved the whole time. Lowell and Miriam loved the city. Their marriage was better than ever, but Seth was miserable. They let him come to the ranch that first summer and every year after that. He came to stay as soon as he finished college and never left. Ranching is the only thing he's ever wanted to do. Two years ago when my Harry died, Seth used an inheritance from his grandfather to buy the place back. Funny, but the old man was the only one who understood what the place meant to him. I think Seth's parents always expected him to give up his dream and settle in the city.''

"They must not know him very well," Janna murmured. "He'd never give up his home—or anything else that was important to him."

Emmie's brows rose. "You figured that out a lot quicker than most people."

Blushing, Janna pushed her hair back from her face. She wasn't about to tell Emmie exactly how much time she spent thinking about him. "Even in a week you can learn a lot about Seth Brody."

"And I bet you've learned that he never plans to marry—and now you know why. Mind you, I'm not convinced he wouldn't change his tune if he could find someone who likes the life there. Someone who'll put up with the hard work and the loneliness."

Janna grinned teasingly. "And you thought Melinda Crandall might be that person?"

Emmie shrugged. "I can hope, can't I? How can he meet anyone when he hardly ever gets off the ranch? He may have to import a bride."

"Don't look at me!" Janna held her hands up, palm outward. "He's already told me—emphatically, I might add—that he won't marry."

"Poppycock."

Janna didn't meet Emmie's shrewd gaze, when she said, "Well, he definitely won't marry someone who might take him away from the ranch. I guess he's afraid of the risk."

"You've got that right. It's a common cowboy problem."

"What do you mean?"

"I've got this theory," Emmie began thoughtfully, "developed from years of hanging around cattlemen. They don't like anything, even a woman, that takes them off their ranch, whether they own it or not. Also, they may be married, but they never *look* married."

Janna laughed. "How can someone look married?"

"Most married men look like they've got people depending on them, and they depend on people. A cattleman doesn't. He's used to working alone, being alone, depending on himself. There's something about him that can't be subdued or tamed by animals, circumstances or people. That's why he's so much a part of our national identity. Men admire him and women want to change him.''

"I see," Janna murmured, thinking of Seth. Everything Emmie said fit him exactly, and it was a clear warning that she shouldn't try to change him.

They talked about other things after that. Emmie gave Janna many suggestions on roundup cooking, what to have prepared ahead of time, and how to make coffee over a camp fire. Janna took careful notes, wrote down a few recipes that Emmie recited from memory, and departed with her head reeling with the number of things she needed to know—and the story of the Brody family.

A lot of things were clear now. Seth might be attracted to her, but he wouldn't pursue it. As far as he was concerned, she was only at the Diamond B Ranch temporarily. If she told him how much she was coming to love the ranch, things might be different.

In order to explain her feelings about ranch life, though, she might have to explain what her home in California was like and that led to her next dilemma.

Seth knew about her broken engagement and the argument with her father, but she'd never gone into detail. Thank goodness, he hadn't asked. She'd let Seth think she was desperate for a job because she was destitute. While she hadn't exactly lied, she hadn't been free with the truth, either, and that's the way Seth would see it. He might even feel embarrassed by his offer of a plane ticket home. Although he wasn't arrogant, he was proud and he wouldn't like being embarrassed.

If asked to pinpoint the moment when she'd stopped being irritated with men, she couldn't have done so. In spite of the tension between Seth and herself, she had tremendous respect for him. She had never seen anyone work as hard as he did.

With a discouraged sigh, Janna wondered why she couldn't seem to remember that she was at the ranch to prove herself and help out until both Emmie and Sue were recovered. She was not there to get involved with the boss.

"JANNA, ARE YOU ready yet?" Seth bellowed from the front hall. "José and the boys have already left."

"I'm coming!" Janna capped her lipstick and stepped back from the mirror to give her appearance one last critical survey. She had pulled her hair back on one side with a big gold clip and left the rest loose.

The peach dress had been a good choice because it showed off the tan she was acquiring, especially with the wide, elasticized neckline pulled down to expose her shoulders. As accessories, she wore her new gold hoop earrings that dangled almost to her collarbone, and her gold necklace. She looked somewhat gypsyish, but she thought it suited her.

Satisfied at last, she hurried out to the kitchen, picked up the chocolate cake she had carefully baked and placed in a plastic cake carrier, then headed toward the front hall.

"Janna!"

"Here I am," she declared, sweeping into the room, her high-heeled sandals clicking on the hardwood floor.

Seth, who had been checking his watch for what she was sure was the umpteenth time, spun around when she spoke. "Well, it's about damned time."

"I don't know why you're so worried. It doesn't start for fifteen minutes, and... What's the matter?"

He was staring at her as if she'd grown two heads. His eyes glittered as his gaze swept to her toes, then up to her face. The corner of his mouth crimped downward.

Uncertainly, she set the cake on the hall table, then straightened and looked at herself. "It's the dress, isn't it? It's not right."

He swallowed before he spoke. "It's fine."

"Are you sure?" She didn't know why she was so worried. She certainly knew how to dress. After all, fashion ruled her hometown.

The way a person dressed didn't seem to matter here, but this was a big annual event. She didn't want to be an embarrassment to Seth. He was different than the men she usually went out with—not that this was a date, of course.

She eyed him anxiously, not sure what was troubling him. She noticed he was dressed up, too. He wore crisp black jeans and a western-cut shirt in a shade of dark green that made him look sexy and dangerous. Around his neck was a bolo tie with a polished malachite clasp. In his hand was a tan Stetson she'd never seen before.

"I have another dress." She chewed her lip. "No, that won't work, it's silk."

"I said the dress is fine." He walked over to her. "Except for one thing." He put his hat on his head, and his dark brown eyes regarded her from beneath its shadowy brim. Lightly grasping the puff sleeves of her blouse, he tugged them up over her shoulders. "Let's not give the local boys too much of a thrill, okay?"

She shivered at the touch of his hands on her shoulders and looked at him in startled delight, for some reason liking the possessiveness she heard in his voice. Her own voice was husky when she answered, "Okay."

"As it is, nobody's going to believe you're just my housekeeper." He turned to open the door for her.

Calling herself a fool, Janna stared at him for a moment, then scooped up the cake and strolled out the door. What else had she expected? The other day she'd spent the entire drive back from Safford thinking about what Emmie had said and reminding herself why a relationship between her and Seth wouldn't work. Things certainly hadn't changed.

While Seth locked the front door, Janna descended the steps and started for the truck, which he had parked by the gate. A blur of movement came at her from the right, and she froze. Since Seth had warned her about rattlesnakes, she'd jumped at every unexpected shadow in the rosebushes. This was no snake, though—it was Jackhammer, and her beady little eyes were trained on Janna's feet. Janna stood still an instant too long, allowing the hen to dart up and give her a painful peck.

"Ouch! You little beast," she shouted, jumping backward. "Get away from me."

But Jackhammer charged forward again, so Janna turned and vaulted over a bush, somehow managing to hold onto the cake.

"Hey, what's the matter?" Seth rushed down the walk.

"It's that blood-hungry chicken of yours! She attacked me."

"How'd she get out? Did you leave the henhouse open?" He swept off his hat and began waving it at Jackhammer in an attempt to shoo her away from Janna.

"Do you think this is the right moment to assign blame?" Janna feinted left just as Jackhammer approached from behind an American Beauty bush.

"You've got to learn how to control these animals." Seth took another swipe at the hen, who ignored him and continued to pursue Janna.

"Me?" Janna shouted furiously, hustling out of the way. "I'm only the housekeeper, remember?"

Squawking loudly, Jackhammer scooted under another bush and hit her target.

"Ouch!" Trying to maintain her balance and keep her grip on the cake plate, Janna kicked out at the hen, who took the opportunity to peck her again.

Seth ran up and put his booted foot between Janna and the chicken. "Head for the truck!"

"What do you think I've been trying to do?"

Jackhammer dashed between Seth's feet, straight at Janna. He waved his hat at her once more, but it snagged on the thorns of the American Beauty. "Damn!"

While he was untangling it, Janna stumbled into him. He straightened abruptly, jostling her elbow. She made a grab for the cake, which miraculously remained upright, but her skirt brushed against the rosebush. Seth's hat fell to the ground. Off-balance and unable to see where she was going, Janna planted her foot squarely on the crown.

With both hands now free, Seth managed to capture the chicken, holding her beak in one hand and her feet in the other.

Finally able to catch her breath, Janna looked down. "Oh, Seth, your hat." She bent to pick it up. The crown was squashed flat, with a noticeable indentation where the heel of her shoe had been. "I'm so sorry."

"Not as sorry as this chicken's going to be. We're having her for dinner tomorrow night—and I don't mean as a guest."

"You're going to *kill* her?"

His jaw dropped. "You mean you want to spare her life? Are you crazy?"

"Maybe she can be trained to..." She trailed off when she saw his expression. "Then again, maybe not." She sighed. "Why don't you lock her in the henhouse for now, and we'll decide what to do later?"

"*We'll* decide? It's my chicken."

"And you certainly don't want to make a decision like that hastily, do you?"

He blew out his cheeks in exasperation. "Has anyone ever told you that you're a managing sort of woman?"

She smirked and started away. "Yes, but I try not to let it go to my head. I'll wait for you in the truck."

"You do that." Carrying his hat and the cake, Janna climbed into the truck and searched through the glove compartment for the small first-aid kit Seth kept there. By the time Seth returned, she had doctored her wounds and was trying to straighten out his hat.

He slid behind the wheel and gave his battle-scarred Stetson a mournful look. "It was brand-new."

"I know. You looked very handsome in it," she told him gravely.

He didn't react to her compliment. "Now it looks like the one Festus Hagen wore on *Gunsmoke*."

Janna couldn't suppress a grin. "No, it looks like it was worn by Festus's horse."

"Yeah," Seth agreed, his tanned face as sad as a little boy who'd just broken his new Christmas toy.

They stared at each other for a few seconds, and then they were laughing together.

"Lord, that chicken hates you, Janna. It's as if she has a personal grudge against you." He turned to her, his eyes gleaming wickedly. "You should have seen yourself jump over that rosebush. Maybe you should enter the Olympics."

"Gold medal rosebush jumper?"

"We could have Jackhammer chase you in case you slow down."

That set them laughing again. Finally, Seth pulled out his handkerchief and handed it to her. She dabbed at her eyes, then slid over next to him and twisted the rearview mirror around to make sure her mascara wasn't running down her cheeks. Satisfied with her appearance, Janna started moving back across the seat bench, but he caught her arm.

"Sit here."

Laughter and warmth lingered on his face. The tension that had been between them over the last few days evaporated, and she smiled back. "Okay."

As she balanced the cake on her lap, he started the engine and pulled out onto the road. Within a few minutes, they had reached the home of Carol and Rob Burnside. The yard was crowded with vehicles so Seth parked down the road.

"Everyone on the creek comes to this and to Emmie's Christmas get-together," he told her. "We dance, and the women swap recipes while the men swap lies, then we all eat too much and go home."

"Sounds like fun." In fact, it sounded like the best of the parties her parents had. Contrary to what most outsiders thought, the intimate parties in Hollywood were attended by nice people who spent the evening talking about their homes and families.

Seth took her hand and tucked it into the crook of his elbow.

She gripped the hard muscles of his biceps. "I thought you were afraid people wouldn't believe I'm really your housekeeper."

He stopped and looked down at her. "I don't care anymore. Do you?"

Her smile could have lit up the night. "No, not at all."

With a nod, he led her to the Burnside's patio where the party was being held. The place was full of people, and loud country music was playing on the stereo. Many couples were dancing, but a number were just standing around talking. Little kids played tag among the adults. Occasionally, a mother would admonish them to take their game into the yard, but the children would dart away with no response.

It was a happy, homey scene. Seth drew her forward to be introduced to their host and hostess.

Rob Burnside was tall and lean, much like Seth, but his eyes twinkled with merriment. Carol was petite and looked plain until she smiled, which she did often. She gave Janna a hug, asked after Emmie, pressed drinks on her two new guests, then rushed away to change the music. José came up to ask Janna to dance, then twirled her away in a wild, stomping step that had her blood pumping and her head whirling. Janna was surprised to discover that the usually quiet man had so much energy in him. Seth laughed at her, then went off to talk to some of the men.

Janna danced two dances with José, then one with each of the Collins boys. Finally, she was able to plead exhaustion and sit down. Seth brought her more punch which she drank gratefully.

"The next slow one's mine," he told her with a smile that sent a rush of heat over her already flushed face.

"All right."

Seth stood beside her for a few seconds, glancing furtively at the group of men he'd just left. She finally realized he wanted to be with them. Smiling fondly at him, she said, "Seth, you don't have to entertain me. Go back to your friends." Her voice was full of teasing. "Why don't you tell them your new method of treating foals with neck injuries?"

He grimaced. "I don't have to tell them. They already know. What do you think they're laughing about over there?"

"I can't imagine," she answered innocently.

With a look that said he would deal with her later, Seth returned to the group of men. Watching them, Janna remembered what Emmie had told her about cattlemen. They really *didn't* look married, especially when they were standing in a group of their peers. Their emotional attachment to their families might be bone-deep, but nothing much interfered with their independence and individuality.

Somehow Janna knew a cattleman wouldn't be caught dead at a meeting of the local parent/teacher organization. But if someone harmed his child, he would be at that school door before first light. All of the men in the group with Seth looked like him—lean and tough. And they had to be, because ranching was hard. She wondered if they hid their deepest emotions so they wouldn't be distracted or weakened by them.

If what Emmie said about the loyalty of the Brody men was true, that was another reason Seth wouldn't marry. He wouldn't leave his ranch for a woman, and if he loved a woman who wouldn't live on the ranch, he couldn't let her go. Because she saw no way around the dilemma, Janna pushed it from her mind, turned to Mrs. Berk, who was sitting near her, and asked how a chiropractor had come to live in the White Mountains.

Seth was as good as his word. When the next slow tune was played, he came and got her from the group of women who had joined her and Mrs. Berk.

They danced with the stars over their heads and a row of sand and candle-filled paper bags, called *luminarias* at their feet. The dance was slow and dreamy and Janna gave herself up to the wonder of it, feeling safe in Seth's arms and knowing she was as close to falling in love as she had ever been.

When the song was over, they filled their plates from a table that groaned under the weight of the food it held and sat down to eat with the Burnsides.

Later, Janna carried a stack of plates into the house for Carol, then found herself standing in the living room admiring a wall full of paintings. They all had Western themes and reminded her of the best of Georgia O'Keefe and Remington. The colors were bold, and the paintings depicted people fighting to succeed against the elements.

One of the paintings featured Seth, standing in the corral, swinging a rope over his head in preparation for lassoing a horse that trotted arrogantly away. Seth appeared determined to catch the animal and control it. Janna recognized that expression and shivered at the strength she saw in him—not just in body, but in spirit, which the artist had captured perfectly. Janna moved closer to look for the artist's name just as Carol Burnside swept into the room.

"Something wrong?" her hostess asked.

Janna shook her head and stepped back suddenly, feeling foolish for mooning over a painting of Seth. She waved her hand to indicate the wall of artwork. "These are wonderful. Who's the artist?"

Carol blushed. "I confess. I'm the culprit."

"You painted that wonderful portrait of Emmie's husband, didn't you?"

Carol seemed pleased. "Why, yes. It's just a little hobby of mine. I'm strictly an amateur."

Janna ran her fingers back and forth over her necklace as she thought. Making a sudden decision, she turned to the other woman. It might mean that her father could track her down, but she had to let Brian Feddoes know about this. "Believe me, you're no amateur. Would you like to sell your work?"

"Of course."

Quickly, she told her about the gallery in California where she had worked. "I'm going to call the owner tonight and tell him about you. Do you have photos of these?"

Carol was clearly flabbergasted, but her face shone with delight. "Well, no, but I can get some."

"Do that. I'm sure he'll want to represent you once he sees them." Excited, she went to find Seth, who didn't seem as pleased as Rob and Carol.

When their host and hostess had moved away to mingle with their other guests, Seth took Janna's arm and pulled her to a secluded part of the yard. "Are you sure you want to do this?"

She blinked at him. "Of course. She's better than a lot of the artists Brian represents. Her work will sell, believe me."

He shook his head impatiently. "That's not what I meant. If you contact your old boss, he might put pressure on you to call your family. Are you ready to do that? I don't know why you broke your engagement and had a fight with your father, but you weren't ready to go home when I suggested it."

"You were trying to get rid of me then. If I go, it'll be my choice. You do have an alternative, you know. You could just fire me."

His jaw tightened. "No. Emmie would—"

"Don't try to tell me you don't make your own decisions. I know better." Frustrated, she turned and went back to the party, leaving Seth standing on the grass. So much for their truce, she thought, as José swept her into another dance. It hadn't lasted long.

The party wound down by ten. Work was always waiting in the morning, no matter how late the ranchers stayed up the night before.

Seth and Janna drove home in a strained silence and as soon as she entered the house, she headed for the kitchen to call Brian Feddoes.

When Brian heard her voice, he sputtered in surprise. "Janna? Where have you been? Your father's been tearing up the country looking for you. He's going to start hiring bounty hunters pretty soon! Your mother's coming home from Kenya to help find you."

Janna felt a stab of remorse. She hadn't meant to upset everything so much. She only wanted to live her own life. "I'm fine, Brian. I'm in Arizona, and I've found an artist for you." She told him all about Carol Burnside, promising to send photos of her work. She knew that once he had the photos and Carol's address, it would be only a matter of time before her father got the information from Brian and sent someone after her—or came himself.

Nevertheless, when she finished her conversation with Brian, she dialed her home. Their housekeeper answered.

"Fiona? It's me, Janna. Is anybody home?"

"Thank heaven, you called. Your family's been worried sick about you. Hold on, I'll get your dad."

"Janna?" Ben shouted when he came on the line. "Where the hell are you? I'll send Alden to pick you up and bring you home."

CHAPTER EIGHT

JANNA GRIPPED THE PHONE with both hands. "No, Dad, I'm not coming home. I've got a job that I like very much, and I'm happy here. So—how are you and Mom? Did Jeffrey and Jeremy go on their camping trip?"

"Camping trip! How could anyone go on a camping trip after you disappeared like that? We thought you'd been kidnapped."

Wearily, she leaned against the wall and rubbed her knuckles across her forehead. "Dad, wouldn't kidnappers have demanded a ransom?"

"Well, maybe," he blustered. "If this had been a normal situation, but there's nothing normal about it."

"You're darned right about that." Out of the corner of her eye, she could see that Seth had propped himself against the doorjamb and was eavesdropping shamelessly. She sent him a furious scowl and turned her back.

"Come home this instant, Janna Shea. I mean it. This is where you belong. Feddoes says you can have your old job when the remodeling's done and he's ready to reopen. Until then, you can go on a vacation. I'll buy you a ticket to Tahiti, or even a couple of tickets. You and Michael can go. He's agreed to take you back."

She sprang away from the wall. "*What?* Take me back! Dad, he was with another woman—in bed! The bed *I* bought in what was supposed to be our new home! I wouldn't have him back if he was gold-plated and had ruby-studded teeth. I can't believe you've even talked to him. If you had any loyalty to me, you would have fired him."

Obviously aware he'd gone too far, Ben began to make amends. "Well, honey, I did fire him. He showed up for work the next morning like nothing had happened, so I picked him up by the scruff of the neck and threw him out of the office. Fired his secretary, too."

The image of her burly father tossing Michael onto the street raised her spirits, although she realized she didn't care as much as she had before she'd come to the Diamond B. "Thanks, Dad."

"When you didn't call, I thought maybe you still loved him so I phoned him. I was only trying to do what's best for you."

"Getting reengaged to him certainly wouldn't be that. Dad, please don't interfere." Realizing how she must sound, Janna fought to control her temper. "Dad, I'm making a new life for myself. I don't need you to run things for me. I'm twenty-three. I can handle my own life."

"You can do that at home!" His domineering nature was apparently overcoming his patience.

She was almost crying now, from homesickness and from frustration. Why wouldn't he listen to her? "No, Dad, I can't. I've found a job that I love in a place that I love. It's peaceful here, and...and the people are wonderful. I feel like I'm needed."

"Your place is with your family!"

"My place is where I make it. But that doesn't mean I don't love you—" Her voice broke, and she didn't think she could take much more. "I've got to go. Kiss Mom for me and say hi to Jeff and Jem. I love you, Dad."

"Janna! Janna, don't you hang up...." Ben was still shouting into the phone when she quietly set the receiver back on the hook. She leaned her head against it and let the tears flow. Nothing had changed. He was still determined to run her life.

She heard Seth's boots as he crossed the floor, then he was turning her into his arms. She tried to swipe the tears from her face and pull away. "I'll get your shirt all wet."

"Hush, Janna. The shirt doesn't matter." He let go of her long enough to fish in his back pocket for his handkerchief, which he pressed into her hand.

She really cried then, sobbing furiously while he held her. "He doesn't understand. He doesn't even listen. He just wants to control my life."

"Maybe he doesn't want you to get hurt. If I had a daughter, I'd feel the same way. I'd horsewhip anyone who tried to hurt her."

Janna looked up through tear-swollen eyelids and recalled all the times she'd compared Seth to her father. She also had a fleeting image of a tiny girl with his dark hair and eyes. "I don't doubt that for a minute."

He grinned briefly, his serious expression changing into one of boyish mischief. But then the smile faded, and his face grew serious again.

Janna trembled when he rested his hand against her throat. Her pulse hammered against his palm as he ran his thumb over the tiny cleft in her chin, then along her bottom lip.

In the past few days, she had been battered and buffeted by so many emotions that she wasn't sure she could trust her feelings.

When he lowered his head, Janna reached up to place her fingers over his lips. "Don't do it if you don't mean it," she whispered, pleading.

That stopped him.

With shaking hands, she reached up and wrapped her fingers around his wrists. "If you touch me now, I won't want you to let me go, and someday I'll have to go home and face my father. I'm not ready yet, but I will be. We both know that."

"So we shouldn't start anything we can't finish," Seth added. In his eyes, desire and reluctance warred for control. Finally, he dropped his hands to his sides and stepped away. "You're right. You don't need this."

He was wrong. She needed it—needed him—but she wanted more than just a brief fling. And time was running out; she knew her father. He wouldn't give up looking for her and trying to bring her home.

When he did find her, she'd have to try again to convince him she could take care of herself. Still, she might have to go back with him, which meant leaving Seth. That thought nearly sent her to her knees. If she and Seth made love, she could never leave him. But she wasn't ready to tell him that. He might not want her to stay, especially once he found out about her family.

She wished she'd told Seth the truth about her family. She really should, but couldn't bear to see the warmth and compassion fade from his face. She needed, if not his love, at least his approval.

Seth ran his fingers over her cheek in a gesture of longing and regret that brought her close to tears once more. "Good night, Janna," he said, as he turned and left the kitchen.

Disheartened, she watched him walk away, then went into her own room. Shutting the door behind her, she sat on the neat white bedspread and let her shoulders slump.

Too much had happened to her recently. Too many emotions had battered her. Though it had been a struggle, she'd achieved a small measure of independence. She couldn't let her father take that away. Neither could she risk giving her heart to Seth.

He wanted her, but not because of love.

As for her, she had just been fooling herself. She loved Seth Brody with all her heart. The feelings she'd had for Michael were like a pale mist compared to the love she had for Seth. But love wasn't going to be enough.

Roundup started the next day and although Janna had spent a restless night, she had to be up and ready early. She was learning very quickly that there was no such thing as self-indulgence on the Diamond B Ranch.

After calling Carol Burnside and telling her to send photos of her paintings to Brian, she gathered eggs. On her way back from the henhouse—where Jackhammer still ruled supreme in spite of Seth's threat to wring her neck, Janna saw Seth coming out of the barn. He gave her a quick searching look, as if to assure himself that she was all right, then smiled, said good morning and went about his business. She wasn't sure whether she should feel disappointed or relieved. The discovery of her true feelings for him was too raw and new, and she wasn't ready to explore it yet. They were going to go back to being employer and employee if it killed her.

They rushed through an earlier-than-usual breakfast, then José helped her load lunches, bottles of ice water and a big, fire-blackened coffeepot into the truck. Seth and the other men wrestled a portable fence into the truck bed, then added boxes of supplies. With José driving, they started off, the battered vehicle bouncing over rough ground to the pasture where they would begin work. The men rode on ahead, with Gus and Steve leading Hildy and José's horse, a well muscled pinto.

Once they reached the pasture, they set the fence up in a circle that formed two small corrals and started up a butane burner on which to heat the coffee and the branding irons. With José's help, Janna set the coffee on to boil, then picked up one of the irons. It was heavy, and it had the ranch's brand on the end—a diamond with a large B in the center.

Shuddering at the thought of the painful burn the calves were going to receive, Janna set the branding iron down and wiped her hand on her jeans.

"It stops hurting in a couple of days, you know." Seth spoke from behind her.

"Tell that to the calves."

"They wouldn't believe me."

"And neither do I."

He grinned and the tension between them eased a bit. "We'll only be branding the few calves we missed in the spring. They've also got to be inoculated. I want you to handle that."

Janna blanched. "Seth, I know I'm supposed to say I can do it—just like I always do—but sticking a needle into an innocent little calf?"

"Innocent? Wait'll you see them. They're all bigger than you, and you won't be thinking innocent when they try to kick you."

She clamped her hands onto her hips. "If they're so hefty, how do you expect me to hold them down while I inoculate them?"

"We'll hold them down. You just do the vaccinating."

Janna sighed. "Oh, all right." She glanced around the empty pasture. "Where are they?"

He laughed again. "Do you expect them to waltz up and say, 'Here I am'? We have to go find them. That's why it's called roundup."

Janna gave Seth an irritated look and lifted her chin proudly. "I knew that."

"Sure you did." He swung into Mexico's saddle and waited for her. She gathered Hildy's reins and mounted, congratulating herself on how well she had learned to ride. Seth spurred his horse, and Janna followed confidently.

Nearby, Gus and Steve smothered their laughter and rode off with José. Barker stayed behind to tend the butane burner and heat the brands, since they had to be ready when the first cattle were driven in. After lunch, he would trade places with Gus.

In no time at all, Janna discovered that riding Hildy around the yard was far different than riding over rough terrain, searching for cows.

She had always considered herself strong. After all, she was quite healthy and had spent the past winter working out at a trendy health club, learning to lift weights. By midmorning, though, her arms felt as if they were going to drop off, and her leg muscles were screaming for mercy.

She was too stubborn to let Seth know she was suffering, so she toughed it out, trying to move with Hildy's rhythm and remain upright in the saddle.

Janna cast Seth a resentful look. He sat easily in the saddle, perfectly comfortable, as if he was in the one place in the world he wanted to be. He let Mexico move at a fast walk while he checked the ground for cattle tracks. Janna tried to keep up as best she could, wondering why he could possibly want her along. So far, she'd done nothing but try to stay in the saddle. Exasperated, she finally asked him.

"Wouldn't it have made a lot more sense if you'd brought Barker along and left me to tend the burner?" she groused, stiffening her legs in the stirrups so she could lift herself up to ease some of the strain on her bottom. "I don't even know what I'm looking for."

Seth glanced back at her. Automatically, she dropped into the saddle and tried to look like an expert horsewoman. The pain made her wince.

"I brought you along so you could learn something."

"Oh, joy," she muttered.

"And so I could listen to the sweet things you always find to say to me." He paused and leaned out of the saddle as he studied the ground, then pointed to some tracks. "Here we go. Can you keep up?"

"Of course."

"If you can't, all you have to do is say so."

Not on your life, she thought, but she said, "Let's get on with it."

They really moved then, until they spotted a cow and her calf in the shade of a stand of aspens. Seth circled them and began urging them the way he wanted them to go. Before they found the cows, they'd been trotting, but now they were just ambling.

Janna sighed in frustration and twisted in the saddle. Although she'd borrowed one of Emmie's hats so that the sun would be off her face, she was feeling hot and thirsty. "It's going to take us forever to get back. Can't we speed this up?"

Seth looked at her as if she'd suggested murder. "Good Lord, no. Cows gain weight slowly and lose it fast. I won't make any profit on skinny cows that have been running up and down the White Mountains."

Resigned, and determined not to complain, Janna settled down to the job. When Seth spotted another cow with two calves, he sent her off after them. She managed to get them headed in the right direction by keeping her horse between them and the way they really wanted to go—which was as far from her as possible.

Seth nodded approvingly as she brought them to him, and she couldn't have felt prouder if he'd handed her a gold medal.

When they reached the portable corrals, Barker jumped up to let them in. Janna watched in admiration as Seth brought Mexico between the two cows and their calves, driving the bawling mothers into one corral and the babies into another. Barker rushed to shut the connecting gate, and Seth rode up to Janna.

He took off his old black hat and removed the dust by slapping it against his leg. "I'll show you how to do the vaccinations. The others should be in pretty soon with more of the herd, and you can do all the calves at once."

"I can't wait," she answered, although the thought of sticking a hypodermic needle into a cow, or anything else, made her stomach lurch.

Seth dismounted and threw his reins over the corral railing, then leaned against a post. He crossed his arms over his chest and regarded her with wicked amusement. "You're my hero, Janna. You're always so cheerful and ready to try anything."

"Yeah, well, right now the only thing I'd like to try is to plant my boot in the seat of your pants."

"You know, I don't think we've got the proper boss/employee relationship working here. The day we met, I told you that you had to learn some basic subservience."

She shrugged, a smile glimmering on her lips. "I've never been very good at that sort of thing."

"No kidding. By the way, if you're going to kick me in the pants, you'll have to get down off that horse first."

Darn! How had he known she was stalling for fear her exhausted muscles would give out when she tried to stand? Defiantly, she eased Hildy up close to Mexico, slung her leg over the pommel in a careless manner and jumped to the ground. By some miracle, she didn't collapse. While her watery muscles adjusted to her weight, she stalled for a few minutes more, patting and whispering to Hildy. When she thought she could walk without falling, she let go of the horse, tossed Hildy's reins over the rail and swaggered triumphantly over to Seth's side. Then proceeded to trip over a rock. If Seth hadn't been quick, she would have landed on her nose.

He held her in his arms and grinned down at her. "You'd die before you'd admit you can't do something, wouldn't you?"

Never in her life had she wanted anything as much as resting her head against his shoulder and staying where she was for a year. Instead, she pushed away from him. "I wouldn't die exactly."

"You'd suffer a lot." He shook his head as he let her go. "Come on, there's work to be done. We've got to catch a calf, vaccinate and brand him, then let him join his mother."

"Sounds easy enough."

"We've got to catch him, first."

Janna expected him to get back on Mexico and rope the calf the way she'd seen rodeo cowboys do it on television. However, he held the gate and ushered her through, calling for Barker to bring the vaccine. He handed them a square black box before returning to the burner to wait for Seth to ask him to bring the branding iron when he needed it. Janna discovered that the more she moved around, the better she felt, so she figured she would be able to handle the next phase of the operation. Seth flipped the insulated box open and pulled out an inoculation gun.

She glared at him. "You deliberately let me think I'd have to stick a syringe into these poor things, didn't you?"

"Let's say I like to watch you squirm."

"You're a rat, Seth Brody."

"I know," he said with a smirk. "It's one of my more endearing qualities."

She laughed at his teasing, even as she wondered if he was trying to make things easier for her after her emotional storm of the previous night. If he was, she was grateful for his sensitivity.

Seth showed her how to load the vaccination ampule into the gun, telling her she would have to press it to the calf's hide and pull the trigger. He removed the ampule and made her practice over and over. It looked simple enough, and she knew it probably wouldn't hurt, but Janna was still reluctant to do it. Nevertheless, Seth was depending on her. When he thought she was ready, Seth chased a calf down and flipped him onto his side. "Janna, come on."

She rushed to him, vaccine gun in hand, and knelt opposite him over the prone body of the frightened little calf. It rolled its big brown eyes in terror and bawled for its mother, who bawled back. Hearing its mother, it surged upward, trying to get away. But Seth wrestled the struggling calf down again.

Pitying the poor creature, Janna hesitated.

"What are you waiting for, Janna? Give him the shot."

"Oh, sorry." She aimed it exactly as Seth had shown her. Just as Janna was about to pull the trigger, the calf fought once again, so Seth threw his arm across the animal and held it. Janna closed her eyes and squeezed as hard as she could.

"*Yeow!* Janna, will you watch what you're doing?"

Her eyes flew open to see that Seth had fallen back in the dirt and was clutching his forearm. The calf, now free, raced away to huddle against the fence as close to its mother as possible. "What happened?"

"You got *me* instead of the calf!"

"No! Oh, Seth I'm sorry." Horrified, she scrambled over to him. Batting his hand away, she examined his arm. The vaccination didn't appear to have broken the skin, but it worked through cowhide, so surely it could penetrate human skin. What would the medicine do to humans, anyway? Something horrible, no doubt.

"What can I do? Is this going to make you sick? Is there an antidote?" she asked frantically.

He gave her a sharp look. "An antidote? I don't—" He broke off suddenly and closed his eyes. His voice trembled. "No. There's nothing anyone can do. It's just a matter of time."

"*Nothing?*"

Behind them, Barker turned to carry the branding iron back to the fire. "Looks like you won't be needing this for a while," he observed.

Appalled by the cowboy's callousness, Janna started to berate him, but Seth clutched her hand. "This is my fault. What can I do? I'll do anything for you, Seth."

"You can kiss me."

"*What?* How will that help?"

But he only said, "Kiss me like you mean it."

"We can't waste time kissing when you need to get to a doctor."

"Kissing is never a waste of time," he murmured, drawing her downward.

Exasperated, she brushed her lips lightly against his. "There."

"Not like that. A real kiss."

Since she was no match for his strength, she kissed him again, putting all the love she had for him into it. It was passion she'd never shown him before, all the love and warmth in her heart pouring out to enfold him.

Janna held him tightly, letting her feelings for him swell as her lips met his. Her heart was pounding in her ears, and she could feel his hammering in his chest.

They could smell each other—a hint of soap, the dust and grass of the makeshift corral and the animals in it.

They could taste each other—the sweetness of their mouths, the saltiness of their skin.

Janna lifted her head. She knew he could read her love for him in her eyes, but she didn't care. She could no longer deny it. She thought she saw the same in his, but, afraid she was projecting her own feelings onto him, she closed her eyes and kissed him again.

"Listen, you two, I'm as much in favor of love as the next man, but the boys are coming in with some more of the herd so you might want to get up from there."

Hazily, Janna broke the kiss, trying to focus on Barker. He was leaning on the fence, watching them with a knowing expression on his face.

She blinked and shook her head to clear it, then glanced behind Barker to see José and the Collins boys approaching with a bunch of cows. She bit her lips, which still tasted of Seth.

"We've got to get you up. . ." She didn't finish, because Seth calmly jumped to his feet, then hauled her up beside him. He dusted both of them off with quick, efficient strokes of his hands.

"Yeah, I know. Those guys have lousy timing, don't they? I ought to fire them."

Her jaw sagged open, then snapped shut. "There's nothing wrong with you, is there?"

His grin was totally male and completely unrepentant. "How could there be? You forgot to load the ampule into the gun."

"I did not! I—" She looked down to see it lying in the dirt beside an indentation made by her knee. She must have dropped it in her haste. She glared at him. "You set me up!"

"It was a chance too good to miss. You weren't even watching what you were doing because you were so afraid of hurting that calf."

She wanted to pound him, but instead, she reached out and poked him in the chest. He yelped, then laughed at her fury.

"You let me think you were sick."

"I never said that. I just let you draw your own conclusions."

"All of them wrong!"

He shrugged. "A man has to take whatever opportunities he can."

"I'll say it again—you're a rat, Seth Brody. A dirty, rotten, low-down rat."

He held up a finger like a schoolteacher correcting a student. "No, just an opportunist." He tilted his head and looked at her speculatively. "There's something about being in a dirty, dusty corral with you that turns me on." She would have flown at him, but he caught her, planted a kiss on the end of her nose and said, "Calm down, honey—we've got work to do." While she fumed, trying to think of something truly horrible to do or say to him, he picked up her hat and handed it to her. With a wink, he added, "Now admit it, it was pretty funny."

The golden lights in his dark eyes invited her to laugh with him, to share the joke on herself. As much as she wanted to stay angry with him, she couldn't quite manage it. She burst out laughing and slapped him with her hat before she plunked it back onto her head.

"I'm going to get you for this, Seth, just you wait and see."

"I'm breathless with anticipation."

"Smart aleck," she accused affectionately.

"Guilty," he agreed, turning away to climb back on Mexico. Then he started cutting the calves from their mothers.

Janna gathered up the box of vaccine equipment and scampered out of the way, grinning foolishly as she watched him work.

What had that kiss meant? It was as if all his reserve had dropped away since yesterday—no, since last night. He seemed to want her as much as she wanted him. Did that mean he wouldn't pressure her into going home? Was there a possibility he might come to accept her as a permanent part of his life?

Pipe dreams, her common sense told her, but her soaring heart just wouldn't listen.

CHAPTER NINE

By six o'clock that evening, Janna realized she had never before known the meaning of the word "tired." They'd found fifty calves that needed to be vaccinated, branded and, for the bull calves, castrated. The six of them had worked flat-out for eight hours, taking only a half-hour break to eat the lunch she'd packed.

Janna found the whole process bloody and barbaric. She admitted she'd led a sheltered existence, but she'd never imagined such cruelty was committed by cattlemen.

She was dizzy from the heat and smoke, nauseated from the smell of burning flesh and hair—and disgusted by the whole process.

"Branding is cruel," she told Seth as they were packing up to leave. The calves and cows were to be kept in the pen until the next morning when José would check their brands, spray them with disinfectant once again, then let them go. "Don't try to tell me that it doesn't hurt them, because they wouldn't cry out like that if it didn't."

Seth slung the branding irons into the back and nodded his head in agreement. "Yes, it does hurt, but we have to be able to mark them somehow. All of the ranchers around here use the same range land. We try to keep our herds separate, but there's almost always a fence down, or a gate left open, or something. If we didn't brand them, we wouldn't know who was whose.''

"It's still cruel." She gave Hildy's reins to Gus and prepared to get into the cab.

Laughing, Seth leaned on his saddle horn. "If it bothers you, why don't you find some other way of marking them."

"Maybe I will. I could do it, you know."

"I don't doubt that for a minute." He gave her a shrewd look. "We could notch or tag their ears."

"That would hurt, too," she protested. She rubbed the back of her dusty hand across her nose as she thought the problem over. "We could paint their hooves a certain color."

"And dab a little perfume behind their ears to make them smell better. Now why didn't I think of that?"

She stuck her tongue out at him, and he laughed again. Pulling on Mexico's reins, he started away. "I'll meet you back at the house."

Janna waved her hand at him and slumped against the seat, grateful José was driving. Although the older man had worked harder than she had, he hardly seemed winded. As they headed home, she watched Seth widening his lead before them.

Something had changed between them. Since he'd tricked her that morning, she'd seen less wariness in him. Now he treated her with the same easy affection

he had for Emmie. But there was also an undercurrent of attraction and sexual awareness. She didn't
know what had caused it, or how long it would last.
The whole thing mystified her, but she was going to
enjoy it without questioning it.

As she was lost in this happy daydream, José said to
her, "I've worked here for ten years, and I've never
seen Seth this happy."

She turned to him in surprise. "You think he's
happy?"

"Of course. He's never let a woman stay around for
long, although Señora Carr has paraded many pretty
girls before him." José's eyes twinkled in his grizzled
face. "And he's sure never had trouble keeping his
hands off one before."

Face flaming, Janna looked away, but she couldn't
help smiling.

Once they reached the ranch, the men began cleaning their equipment in preparation for the next day.
Janna knew she should have started cooking dinner
right away, but her clothes were manure-spattered,
bloodstained and filthy. So she headed for the shower.

Twenty minutes later, damp hair streaming down
her back, and dressed in fresh clothes, she was getting
out the ingredients to make biscuits to accompany the
stew she'd left simmering in a huge crockpot. Seth
passed through the kitchen, stopping to swing her hair
out of the way and kiss the back of her neck before he
headed upstairs for a shower. If her skin hadn't been
holding her together, she would have melted all over
the countertop like warm honey.

Mouth agape, she stared after him, her heart full of shock and her hands loaded with cans of baking powder and shortening.

He stopped in the doorway. "Janna, I'll be sleeping in the bunkhouse from now on."

She blinked. "The bunkhouse? Why?"

A slow, sexy grin hitched up one side of his mouth. "I think you know." He turned and, whistling, made his way upstairs.

Janna slumped against the counter. He was trying to protect her reputation. By some miracle, she'd fallen in love with an honorable man. What good would it do her, though? She'd be leaving soon, going home to face up to her father and her responsibilities. If someday she returned, would Seth want her back? He hadn't indicated that he loved her—only desired her. And what if he saw her leaving, no matter how good the reason, as an echo of his mother's dislike for the isolation of Fawn Creek? Realizing she had no answers, only questions, Janna went back to work.

After dinner, she cleaned the kitchen and began preparations for the next day, taking a roast beef from the freezer to thaw. She looked at it and shook her head. If she stayed around, she'd have to do something about the diet of these men. It contained far too much red meat. She wondered how they'd feel about pasta. She smiled sadly to herself. Those kinds of thoughts denoted permanency.

She made stacks of sandwiches for the next day's lunch, then packed some of the cookies she'd baked in advance.

Carol Burnside called to tell her she'd taken photos of some of her paintings and sent them to Brian Feddoes. Janna knew that he'd soon have Carol's address, which meant he'd have Janna's—and so would Ben. Her days were numbered.

Too tired to worry about it, she went to her room, changed into her nightgown and collapsed into bed.

"COME ON, SLEEPYHEAD. You've got to get up."

A voice drifted into Janna's cocoon of sleep. She ignored it, pulling the sheet up to her chin and snuggling into the one pillow that was left. She halfheartedly searched for the other so she could put it over her head, but she couldn't find it. No doubt it was on the floor where it usually landed during her nightly thrashings.

"Janna, wake up. We've got to get going."

She groaned as she recognized Seth's voice. "Go away. I just got into bed."

"It's seven o'clock," he said relentlessly. "You know what that means, don't you?"

Janna lifted her head, but refused to open her eyes. "It must mean it's time for my funeral. Is your black suit pressed?"

He chuckled. "No. It means you've got to get up. We're waiting breakfast on you."

Now that he mentioned it, she could smell bacon. Enviously, she wondered who had cooked it. She hadn't mastered bacon yet. When she moved to turn over, pain shot through her, and she groaned again.

"Don't wait for me. Dead people can't eat. It's a scientific fact."

Ignoring her protests, Seth picked her up and propped her against the headboard. She moaned once her full weight rested on her bottom. "You're heartless."

"I know. That's why I brought you this. I'm trying to trick you into thinking I'm a heck of a nice guy." He lifted her limp hand and pressed a cup of coffee into it.

The wonderfully inviting smell brought her eyelids to half-mast. Seth was grinning down at her, so devilishly handsome and full of life as he sat on the side of the bed that she said, "It worked. Now, what have you got for aching muscles?"

He stood up. "More riding."

She whimpered.

"Sorry," he replied, not looking the least bit sorry. "But it's the only way. If you stay in bed today, you'll be stiffer than ever."

"Well give me the chance to find that out for myself. I'm willing to make that mistake." She sipped her coffee and considered him. "Do you take bribes?"

"Depends on what kind." Seth took the cup out of her hand and set it on the spooled maple nightstand. Then he picked her up, sheet and all, and sat down on the bed with her on his lap. He looked at her with such warmth that she blushed.

Self-consciously, she smoothed her hair. "I'm a mess."

"You're beautiful." To prove it, he kissed her. Janna slid her arms around his neck and plunged her fingers into his hair, something she'd wanted to do for ages. Kissing him was a better stimulant than caffeine.

When he pulled away, she murmured, "You know, you make a big impression on a girl when you do that."

"Oh, yeah?"

"Uh-huh. In fact, I'd say that you're a world-class kisser. Maybe we should enter *you* in the Olympics. I could be your trainer."

"Ah, but how would you feel when I was actually in a competition?"

"Jealous. Maybe that's not such a good idea. I could just start a Women Who've Kissed Seth Brody Club."

"Believe me, there wouldn't be that many members."

Delighted, she sat up straight. "Really? Why not?"

A hint of pain flashed in his face, and she remembered what José had said about the small number of women who'd been around over the years. "Because I work all the time and have since I was a kid. Because I live in these mountains. There's not many women around, and few who'd want to stay if they came here."

I'd stay, she wanted to shout. *Just ask me.* Instead, she said in a flippant tone, "Well, I don't mind being the only member."

His smile returned. "I'll take your application under consideration. Right now, I can allow you enough time for a hot bath to work the soreness out of your muscles, but you've got to get going."

"There's only a shower in my bathroom."

"There's a tub upstairs."

The tub he used. How silly of her to feel a shiver of anticipation at the thought of using it when she'd been cleaning it for two weeks. "That sounds great," she said. "If I can find the energy to climb the stairs."

"No need." With her in his arms, he surged to his feet.

"Wait a minute!" she squeaked in surprise, clutching at the sheet that covered her.

"Get your robe." He bent so she could snag it from the bedpost, then headed for the hallway.

"Seth! Everybody's out there. What will they think?"

He gave her a look of mock arrogance. "They don't get paid to think. Besides, I'm the boss. I can do whatever I want."

She wrinkled her nose at him.

"Janna, they're too busy eating breakfast. They won't even notice."

"I thought you said they were waiting breakfast on me."

He shrugged as he stepped from her room. "I lied."

She managed to get an arm free so she could pinch him teasingly. He yelped with pain, drawing the attention of the men at the table. They were busily devouring pancakes and bacon that looked better than anything she'd managed to cook for them in the past two weeks. She offered a weak smile. "Good morning, everyone."

José and Barker grinned smugly. Gus and Steve looked on goggle-eyed as she and Seth swept past. When he started up the stairs, she buried her face against his neck. "Seth, I don't know when I've been more embarrassed!"

"You should have gotten up earlier," he answered, unperturbed. "I assume you can handle things from here on?" he asked, setting her on her feet in the bathroom. He flashed a riverboat gambler's grin. "I can stay and help."

And she would be putty in his hands. "Go!"

With a cocky salute, he sauntered out, closing the door behind him.

If she hadn't been so sore, Janna would have danced a jig. She still didn't have a clue as to what had caused Seth's change in attitude, but she was going to enjoy it.

Because they had waited for her to bathe and eat breakfast, which she learned Seth had cooked, they were late reaching the pasture. Janna was grateful they didn't berate her for her sluggishness, and was determined to show what a good ranch hand she could be. She rode with Seth once again, managing to track a cow and calf and flush them from their hiding place. She even herded them back to the holding pen by herself.

When the pen was full, she helped once again and seemed to be developing a rhythm of vaccinating, swabbing ears with tick medicine, pouring worm medicine down the center of their backs and spraying disinfectant on the new brands. She still didn't like the job, but she gritted her teeth and did it.

Grimly, she thought of how horrified her father would be if he could see what she was doing, then felt a moment of sadness. It wouldn't be long before he found her.

By the fourth day of branding, they were nearly finished with the herd, and Janna was quite pleased that she'd survived. She'd learned how to plan ahead, have meals ready and remain cheerful no matter what disaster occurred.

And she discovered that Seth was right about being saddle sore. If she gritted her teeth and forced herself to get onto Hildy's back every morning, her muscles stopped screaming after an hour or so.

On the last day of branding, their pace slowed. Seth figured they'd be finished by noon, leaving the afternoon free. The men were delighted and immediately made plans to go into town. Janna was relieved that branding was over so she could catch up on the regular work around the house. There was more to being a combination of housekeeper and ranch hand than she'd ever imagined. As hard as the work was on the Diamond B, though, she'd miss it when she left.

Even though she wanted to see her family, including her hardheaded father, the thought of returning home depressed her so much that she sighed while she morosely packed away leftover vaccine.

Seth strode up, carrying the butane heater. "Why the long face? Don't tell me you've enjoyed branding so much that you can't stand to see it come to an end?"

Janna smiled ruefully as she put the inoculation gun away. She glanced at Seth, and her heart did a backward somersault.

He was so sexy in his dusty jeans and boots, with the sleeves of his tan shirt rolled up to reveal strong forearms. She loved him more as each day passed, although there'd been no further episodes of him waking her with coffee and kisses.

"I can't say that I'll miss branding, but it's been nice to be out in the open, away from the house. I'll miss this when I go."

His expression became solemn. "You're not going yet. Sue won't be ready to take over for weeks."

Janna knew she didn't have weeks. She may not even have days. As sure as there would be eggs to gather in the morning, she knew her father would do his darnedest to drag her back to California once he found her. She'd proven her point, and he might be more willing to let her run her own life now. The truth was, Janna couldn't stay. She loved Seth, but he didn't love her. He desired her—there was no doubt about that. She read it in his looks, felt it in his touch, but that was no indication he wanted her around permanently.

"I meant I'll miss this place when I do go."

Seth pushed his hat to the back of his head and rubbed his thumb along his jaw as he considered her. "Everyone's going to be gone this afternoon."

"I know. I'd planned to get caught up on the housework."

"Forget that. Come with me. There's something I want to show you."

"What?"

"It's a secret. A surprise." He rocked back on his heels and crossed his arms over his chest.

She'd noticed he assumed this pose when he had something on his mind, usually something good, but she decided to tease him. "Is it a surprise that's going to be painful to me or to any other of God's creatures?"

He grinned. "Nope. Think of it as a date."

"A date?"

"Yeah, you know. One of those occasions when you get dressed up, splash on some of your fancy perfume and make goo-goo eyes at me."

"*Goo-goo* eyes? When was the last time I heard anyone use that expression?"

He lifted his eyebrows in a facial shrug. "So we're a little backward here in the hills. What can I say? Will you come?"

"Yes. Oh, yes, I'd love to."

"Good." He tipped his hat down over one eye and swaggered over to Mexico who was ground-tied nearby. The men had finished loading the portable pens and everyone headed back to the ranch house, eager to take advantage of having the afternoon off.

They drove two dozen yearling calves who were to be picked up by a buyer in the next few days. The men turned them into the corral, gave them plenty of feed and left for town. Janna raced for the shower.

"THIS IS BEAUTIFUL," Janna breathed, pulling Hildy to a stop and looking around the tiny meadow to which Seth had led her. Less than one hundred feet on each side, it was about half a mile from the house and was surrounded by towering pines and aspens. The wind sighed through their branches, sending the aspen leaves into a shivering dance. Fawn Creek ran through one corner of the meadow, tumbling its way downhill to the San Francisco River, then to the Gila and eventually to the Gulf of California.

"The Mexicans called this kind of naturally occurring meadow a *cienega*," he said, putting the accent on the second syllable. "Deer come here, maybe we'll see some." He leaned on the pommel of his saddle and looked around, a slight smile curving his mouth. "I haven't been up here in months. When I was a kid, it was my favorite place to hide out."

"What were you hiding from?"

Seth dismounted, then helped her down. They strolled across the meadow, letting their horses take occasional bites of the knee-high grass. "You name it. My parents' fights, mostly."

Janna slapped the ends of the leather reins against her palm as she sneaked a glance at him, surprised at his openness. "Emmie said something about that."

His smile was swift and sudden. "She's always been protective of me, and she interferes more than I'd like. If she told you about that, she was probably trying to drum up sympathy for me."

"Probably."

"Did it work?"

"Of course." Janna hooked her arm through his. "She said your mother hated it here."

"She did. Still does. My parents live in Phoenix. Hardly ever come up here. I go see them at Christmas and whenever I have business in the city." He paused, and Janna wondered if he was thinking about his childhood. "I was always torn between them. Dad loved the ranch, but Mom hated it. He wanted to be here, but she loved the city. We'd go see her parents and stay for weeks at a time. I hated it after the first few days."

"You wanted to go home."

"Yes, and this was home to me, but never to her. I blamed her then, but I see things differently now. She hadn't been raised here. My grandfather had lots of money and things had always been easy for her. She couldn't adjust. I think she knew that, and I guess what bothered me for years was the feeling that she'd lied to my dad."

A pang of guilt engulfed Janna. "Lied?"

"About being able to live here. I think she always knew she'd talk him into leaving. Now, I think maybe if her life had been harder, she could have lived here just fine."

Janna touched her tongue to the corner of her mouth. "Harder?"

"She'd never had to work, to prove herself in any way. My grandfather's wealth created a cushion of comfort around her. She'd never had to do much of anything before she married Dad. Even she admits she was the worst possible candidate for a rancher's wife." Seth glanced up as if someone had pinched him. "Sorry, you don't want to hear all that."

Janna shifted uncomfortably. She did want to hear it, but her own guilty conscience made it hard for her to listen to him. She took a deep breath and held it for a few seconds. The stalling had gone on long enough. She needed to tell him the truth about her family. While she was thrilled that he thought she was a good worker, there were other misconceptions that she needed to clear up. "Seth, about my family—"

"Look!" He froze, clucking to Mexico to stop while he grabbed Janna's arm. Across the meadow, a bull elk had emerged from the trees to drink at the creek. He had a huge rack of antlers that had red twine twisted in them as if he had broken into a twine-wrapped bale of hay. The string gave him a festive look that was completely at odds with the grandeur of his appearance. He regarded them for a moment before he turned with a flick of his short tail and started off at a leisurely pace as if telling them that he was going—but only because he chose to.

Seth let out a sigh. "Biggest son of a gun I've ever seen. I hope he finds someplace to hide himself during hunting season."

Janna turned and studied him, thinking about the kind of man he was. She thought of how he rode—with an easy rocking motion that seemed to make him one with his horse. He and that elk were alike in their strength and grace.

"What is it?"

"You're like him," she blurted, then blushed a shade of red that clashed wildly with her hair.

"What?" he asked in amazement.

Flustered, she waved her hand and frowned in self-mockery. "Nothing. I'm being silly and corny. Never mind." She started forward again, but he still held her arm. He tugged, bringing her to a stop.

"Tell me what you mean."

She licked her bottom lip. "You're like that elk."

Clearly amused, he said, "*I* am?"

"You always seem to know what you want, where you're going. Even when something takes you by surprise, it doesn't throw you...." Her voice faded away. Oh, Lord, why hadn't she just painted a big sign that read, I Love Seth Brody and nailed it to the side of the barn?

He was looking down at her with such intensity that her heart started to dance crazily. "And what about you, Janna? Do you have an affinity for the land?"

"What do you mean?"

"I heard what you said to your father—that you love it here. Is that true?"

Janna swallowed the lump forming in her throat. "Well, of course, I've enjoyed—"

He dropped Mexico's reins and swung her around until she faced him. "That's not what I asked. Do you love it here?"

"Yes." When she admitted it, her confusion took flight. "Yes. The first time I ever saw this place, I loved it. It's felt like home since the minute I stepped out of your truck."

He sighed, then pulled her against him and kissed her until she tasted, felt, smelled only him.

He finally pulled back and held her away from him. Why had she ever thought his face was harsh and tough? He was looking at her now with love and tenderness that made her want to weep.

"Say it," he commanded gruffly. "Say it."

She spoke through joyous tears. "I love you, Seth."

He closed his eyes and dropped his forehead against hers. "Thank God." He kissed her again.

She was moved to feel his lips trembling against hers as if his emotions were too much for him. She pressed herself against him, wanting to be as close as possible to him. He finally tore away from her, breathing harshly. "Let's go back to the house."

Heat washed from the top of her head to the tips of her toes. They would be all alone in the house, and she knew what would happen—the very thing her fevered imagination had been conjuring since the day she realized she loved him. "All right." She saw the sudden flare of approval in his eyes as she turned away and pulled herself into the saddle.

Recklessness surged through her. She snatched up Hildy's reins and clipped her heels into the mare's sides. "I'll race you," she shouted, and then was off before Seth could get his boot into the stirrup.

The little mare pounded down the path toward home. Janna lay along her neck, urging her forward, laughing when she heard Seth coming up behind her on Mexico. She knew she wasn't a good enough horsewoman for this kind of wild dash, but she didn't care.

She risked a glance over her shoulder and yelped in surprise when she saw how close Seth was. He leaned into the wind, hands gripping the reins, his eyes daring her to beat him.

Janna never turned down a dare. "Come on, Hildy," she urged. "Come on." The mare obliged, giving that extra little burst needed to send them into the ranch yard first.

Janna punched her fist into the air and crowed in triumph, "And the winner is—"

"Only because I held Mexico back," Seth interrupted, jumping down and striding toward her. Janna laughed as he pulled her into his arms. "Trust you to turn my big seduction scene into a romp."

She batted her eyelashes at him, even as she felt the sexual heat beginning to build once again. "It's one of my more endearing qualities."

He hugged her, and they stood with their arms wrapped around each other, content to let their feelings find their own level. He loved her, she just knew it, and any minute now, he would say it.

When their breathing settled, she realized that she was standing on top of his boots. She laughed and pulled his head down for a kiss. "Now I know why the girl did this in *The Friendly Persuasion*. I can reach you so much better this way."

He placed a kiss in her cleft. "I aim to please, ma'am."

Dreamily, she became aware of a loud pulsing sound and drew back to gaze into his face. "Is that your heart?" she teased.

"No, it's—" he glanced up "—it's a helicopter."

Janna gasped and looked up quickly, scanning the sky for what she already knew she would see—the distinctive yellow of the Whitley Corporation helicopter.

CHAPTER TEN

IF SHE HADN'T already known it was her father's heli-copter, all doubt would have been removed by the big black letters emblazoned across the undercarriage.

Seth read them aloud. "Whitley *Corporation?*" He looked at her, puzzled. "Janna, what is this?"

With her face full of dread, she said, "Seth, I can explain."

"Explain?" His expression was incredulous. "Is that some member of your family?"

"Well, yes, actually—" She was interrupted when Hildy, distressed by the noise and wind caused by the helicopter, tried to bolt. Janna fought to hold her, glancing skyward. Her father's pilot, Alden Ford, was obviously having trouble finding a place to land. He must have finally decided on the small meadow be-hind the orchard because the aircraft swung off in that direction.

Seth was having troubles of his own, trying to keep Mexico under control. He finally grabbed both sets of reins and pulled the animals into the barn, shutting the door on them.

Janna trailed after him, watching as he stalked across the yard once again. They had to grab their hats and hold on to keep them from being blown away in the backwash from the rotors.

In the corral, the yearling calves had begun to get restless. Already upset by being separated from their mothers, they were close to panic now. Seeing this, Seth started off at a run, his long legs covering the ground in seconds. Janna was right behind him.

It was too late, though. The cattle surged against each other, hitting the corral fence and splintering enough of the rails to break down one section. Frantic, they pushed through, milling about on the flat ground beside the barn before some of them took off uphill toward the house and others headed downhill toward the road.

"My roses!" Janna shouted in dismay when she saw the group running for the house. The picket fence would be no match for their combined weight. By unspoken agreement, she and Seth split up. He ran after the part of the herd that sensed freedom down the road while she dashed along behind the others. She managed to get ahead of them and, by waving her hat, turned them away from the house. But they scraped too close to the henhouse, destroying the fence that surrounded it.

Jackhammer and her cohorts didn't waste any time. They scrambled through the gap in the chicken wire and ran.

Janna barely noticed them, intent on keeping the yearling calves from annihilating the rose garden. By the time she had them all together, the helicopter's motor had stopped and the rotor blades whined into silence.

She herded the calves back to the barn and met Seth, who looked mad enough to spit nails. He didn't speak as he got the calves back into the corral and secured them there by stringing wire across the broken space. While he was doing that, Janna shooed the chickens back into their enclosure and bent the broken wire together so they couldn't escape.

Meanwhile, her parents had found their way down from the pasture.

As she watched them approach, tears stung the backs of her eyes. She'd missed them so much. She started forward to meet them, but Seth grabbed her arm and swung her around to face him.

"What the hell is going on here, Janna? Who are those people and whatever possessed them to bring that damned machine up here?"

Sick with dread and guilt, Janna faced him. "I tried to explain, Seth, really I did. I just couldn't ever find a good time, and—" she couldn't look at him "—and I didn't want you to hate me for deceiving you."

"Deceiving me?" He said the words like a curse.

But then her parents were there, and her father was sweeping her into a big bear hug. Her mother hugged her, too, then moved back to look at her. "Are you all right, honey?" she asked, anxiously, her eyes focused solely on her daughter. "You had us worried. Your dad's been tearing up the western United States looking for you."

Ben agreed, vociferously. "Damned right. Janna, you had no right to go running off like that, scaring everybody to death." He looked around at the barn, the damaged chicken coop and the corral with its broken fence. "What are you doing here, of all places?"

Janna shook her head. "Mom, Dad, I told you I wanted to get out on my own—"

"Mom and Dad?" A voice thundered near her ear.

She whipped around to see Seth glaring at her. "Uh, I guess I'd better introduce you."

"Why bother?" Seth said through clenched teeth. "I think I've got it figured out."

"No, Seth, you don't," she put in desperately, then swallowed hard when the fierceness of his expression didn't soften. "These are my parents, Ben and Shea Whitley. Mom and Dad, this is Seth Brody, owner of the Diamond B Ranch."

Seth stared at her mother who smiled at him uncertainly. Even without introductions, he, and every other man in America, would have known who she was because of her distinctive red hair, deep green eyes and flawless skin. Shea Willetta Whitley looked years younger than she was, certainly not old enough to have a twenty-three-year-old daughter. Side by side, though, their resemblance was unmistakable.

Ben, on the other hand, looked his age and then some. He was bluff and burly, and his determination and strength of will showed in his every movement. He held out his hand, which Seth gripped briefly before turning to Janna.

"I want to talk to you *alone*." The emphasis on the last word brooked no disobedience.

Ben put a hand on Janna's shoulder. "Now, wait a minute, who do you think you are, talking to my daughter like that?"

Seth's eyes were as dark and lifeless as coal as he looked at Janna. "I'm a fool, that's what I am."

She stepped between the two men while Shea looked on in silent alarm. "It's all right, Dad. Why don't you and Mom go up to the house and wait for me? I'll be right with you."

Although they were both clearly reluctant, Shea dragged Ben away toward the house.

Seth was angrier than Janna had ever seen him. "All right, start with the explanations you were so anxious to give me but could never seem to find the time for!"

With her words stumbling over themselves, she told him about Michael, her father's offer of a vice presidency in the corporation once they were married and Michael's betrayal.

Seth interrupted her. "I know most of that. What I want to hear is why you didn't tell me exactly who your family was. Why did you lie?"

Janna shook her head furiously. "I didn't! You heard me talking to him. You knew he owned a business and . . . and that my fiancé worked for him."

"He could have owned a gas station for that matter. You let me think you were some poor girl with no money or resources. Exactly why did you want this job so badly?"

She was tempted not to look at him, but decided things couldn't get any worse than they already were. "Because I thought my father couldn't find me here. I was determined to prove myself." He snorted in derision and she grew angry, too. She jabbed a finger at him. "You thought it was a good idea. You said you knew what it was like to have to prove yourself!"

"Yeah, but I never deceived anyone while I was doing it. You probably have credit cards that could buy and sell this whole ranch ten times over."

"What if I do? That doesn't change the fact that you needed a housekeeper, and I could do the job."

He gave her a disgusted look. "I needed a housekeeper, yes, but you still could have gotten and kept the job if you'd been honest about what you were running from."

"Oh, really?" she scoffed. "You made it clear from the beginning that you expected me to give up, and I wasn't going to give you that satisfaction."

His face froze into a terrible iciness, and when he spoke his voice dripped with scorn. "Satisfaction? I didn't get any. I've been sleeping in the bunkhouse for the past four nights because I wanted to protect your reputation. Looks like you don't have one that needs to be protected, do you, city girl? Not if you can run from one man to another, spouting lies along the way."

Pain cut so deep she was surprised she wasn't bleeding. She lifted shaky hands to her mouth and when she spoke, her words were whispers. "I didn't lie—not really."

His mouth curled downward. "You expect me to believe what you said a while ago? That you love me? Sorry, only one deceit to a customer and you've used yours up." He started toward the corral. "Pack your things and go. There's nothing for you here."

Hurt and angry, Janna turned toward the house. Tears welled in her eyes, but she brushed them away. Stubborn man! she thought. Why had she fallen in love with such a stubborn man? She certainly wasn't blameless. She should have told him the whole truth days ago, but once she realized she was in love with him, she wanted to preserve their idyllic time as long as possible. Yes, she'd been foolish, but he was impossibly stubborn.

Fuming, she stomped up the porch steps and slammed the front door open, surprising her parents, who jumped up from their chairs and rushed over to her. "Darling, what's wrong?" Shea asked.

"I'm an idiot, that's what's wrong," Janna wailed, then burst into tears.

Shea gathered her close and hustled her to the sofa. Janna sat with her head on her mother's shoulder, relating the whole story. Shea made sympathetic noises while Ben prowled the room offering every few minutes to get Alden to beat the daylights out of Seth.

"Ben, you aren't helping things," Shea admonished him. "If you hadn't interfered in the first place with that disgusting Michael Barrington, none of this would have happened."

"I was just trying to help," he said gruffly. "I didn't want my little girl to make the same mistakes I did."

Janna laughed ruefully and dabbed at her tears. "Too late. I've managed to make a much worse one."

"Do you love this guy? 'Cause there's no waiting period in Arizona, you know. You want to marry him, Alden and I'll hog-tie him and have him in front of a justice of the peace in no time."

"Dad, how did you ever make it in business with this bull-in-a-china-shop personality of yours?"

He didn't seem displeased by her question. "Simple. I never take no for an answer. I never even take maybe for an answer."

"He also carries dynamite for any immovable objects that get in his way," Shea said, looking at him affectionately.

He shrugged. "Works for me." Ben sat down on one of Emmie's delicate chairs, which groaned under his weight. "So, are you going to come home with us?"

"I don't know," Janna admitted, drawing in a steadying breath.

Shea reached up to smooth back Janna's hair. "Does Seth want you to leave?"

"That's what he said." Janna shuddered at the memory of his anger and disgust.

"Do you think he meant it?"

"Oh, yes. I'm sure he did."

"He may have been speaking in the heat of anger," Shea went on thoughtfully. "What does it matter if you're from a wealthy family and your mother's an actress? All you asked for was a temporary job, not a lifetime commitment. To me, it seems like a pretty minor thing to be upset about."

"But not to him."

"Maybe he's reacting this way because his emotions are involved. Would he be this angry if he didn't love you?"

Janna sat up straight. "I don't know."

"Well, hell," Ben snorted. "Are you going to run away again or are you going to stay and find out?"

Janna stared at her parents and felt the first ray of hope she'd experienced for the past hour. Although she still hurt from the things Seth had said, she'd never know whether he truly meant them if she left. Staying would be the ultimate test of her commitment to him.

"I'm not leaving," she stated firmly. "If he wants to get rid of me, he'll have to put me in his truck and drive me out of here himself."

"That's my girl," Shea said with approval as she touched Janna's cheek. "Maybe you've found your career after all."

"Ranch wife? Only if the rancher will have me."

Ben pushed his way out of the creaking chair. "Well, if he doesn't, Alden and I will—"

"No, you won't," Shea insisted, standing and grabbing his arm. "You'll let Janna handle this herself."

He scowled, but his expression softened when he gave Janna a hug. "If you need anything, let us know. And keep in touch. I don't appreciate wasting all this money trying to find you, only to get your address from Brian Feddoes."

"I'll keep in touch, Dad," Janna promised, going up on tiptoe to kiss his cheek. "And if things don't work out, you may see me sooner than you think."

He looked down at her. "I don't think so. You may look like your mother, but you've got my perseverance."

Shea grimaced. "God forbid!"

Laughing, Janna walked them back to the helicopter and waved them off. It was startling to realize that her parents finally saw her as an adult. Maybe that was because she was finally showing them that she was one.

As she returned to the house, she looked around for Seth, but didn't see him anywhere. Her stomach flip-flopped at the idea of facing him, knowing that she'd defied him. She didn't even know what she was going to say. Somehow those three little words, I love you, didn't seem like much defense against his anger.

She'd just entered the house when she heard the pounding of boots on the wooden floor. She reached the doorway between the kitchen and dining room in time to see Seth sweep in from the back hall to snatch up his keys from the countertop.

He skidded to a stop when he saw her, his hand suspended in midair and the keys dangling from his fingers. His face went through swift changes of expression, from disbelief, to hope, to caution. Slowly, he lowered his hand and tucked his keys into his pocket. "You're still here."

Janna's hand crept up to fiddle with her necklace. "That's right."

"I told you to go."

"I ignored you."

"So I see."

He wasn't going to make this easy for her. She lifted her chin. "I have a job to finish, and I'm going to see it through."

"Even if I don't want you here?"

Her lips trembled, but she nodded. "That's right."

"I should have known I couldn't get rid of you that easily." He walked toward her. "You know where I was going?"

She shook her head once, fearfully, as he stopped directly in front of her.

"After you. I heard the helicopter take off, and I decided I'd better get over to Safford and charter a plane."

Her heart was pounding so hard that blood rushed into her face. "So you could come after me?"

"That's right. I acted like the south end of a north-bound donkey."

She smiled at the image. "Yeah, you did."

"And I wanted to apologize." He was standing so close now that they should have been touching. "I overreacted."

She nodded in understanding. "You thought I'd lied and made a fool of you."

He pulled her against his chest. Her arms flew around his neck to hold him tightly, knocking his hat to the floor.

"I was the one who made a fool of myself. You told me you loved me, and I didn't tell you that I love you." He kissed her cheek, her jaw, then finally her mouth. "I knew you were trouble the minute I saw you sitting in that bus depot, but I couldn't resist taking you home, keeping you with me and falling in love with you."

She leaned back to smile shakily at him. "So all that talk about never marrying...?"

"Defense mechanism." He laughed ruefully. "I was a goner the minute you saw this ranch and fell in love with it."

"You knew how I felt about it?"

"Yeah. Your face is easy to read, especially when it's saying exactly what I want to see."

She thumped him on the shoulder. "You snake! You let me fall in love with you and this ranch and think you'd never love me back!" She would have been a lot more angry with him if her heart hadn't been singing with joy.

"Old habits are hard to break. I decided years ago I'd never find anyone who'd love this place like I did."

She pushed her fingers through his hair. "You were thinking of your mother."

He nodded, kissing her once again. "Stupid, isn't it? She did the best she could, but this place wasn't for her. She and Dad were smart enough to figure that out and leave before they started hating each other."

"You were still seeing things as a child would, rather than as a man."

"Yes. I knew you were different because you pitched in and didn't complain. You took care of the roses as if they were your own and when I overheard you telling your father that you loved it here—'' he shrugged ''—I didn't have a chance.''

Janna remembered how his attitude toward her had changed after her conversation with Ben and she leaned her head gratefully against his shoulder. "I love you, Seth, and I love this place. Will you let me share it with you?"

"Only if you'll marry me."

That earned him a breathless "Yes" and an even more breathless kiss. "My dad says there's no waiting period in Arizona."

"He's right." Seth drew back and looked at her. "Sounds like Ben Whitley is going to make one heck of a fine father-in-law."

Her eyes twinkled. "Sure he will, as long as—"

"He doesn't try to run our lives," they cried in unison and then laughed together.

"Somehow I think you're more than a match for him," Janna said.

He grinned. "I'm more interested in being a match for you."

Janna wrapped her arms around him. "Don't worry, you are. You're the perfect match for me."

Let

HARLEQUIN ROMANCE®

take you

BACK TO THE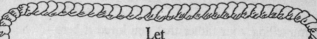

Come to the A-OK Corral, a ranch near Lullaby, Colorado.

Meet Cami "Tex" Greenbush, Texan by birth and wrangler by nature—or so she believes. *And meet* rancher Holt Winston, her new boss, who quickly finds out—to his horror—that Cami can't rope and can't ride. She's a wrangler who's never wrangled!

Read ONCE A COWBOY...by Day Leclaire. It's a laugh-out-loud romance!

Available in February, wherever Harlequin books are sold.

MEN. MADE IN AMERICA

**Fifty red-blooded, white-hot, true-blue hunks
from every State in the Union!**

Look for MEN MADE IN AMERICA! Written by some of our most poplar authors, these stories feature fifty of the strongest, sexiest men, each from a different state in the union!

Two titles available every other month at your favorite retail outlet.

In January, look for:

DREAM COME TRUE by Ann Major (Florida)
WAY OF THE WILLOW by Linda Shaw (Georgia)

In March, look for:

TANGLED LIES by Anne Stuart (Hawaii)
ROGUE'S VALLEY by Kathleen Creighton (Idaho)

You won't be able to resist MEN MADE IN AMERICA!

HARLEQUIN®

Don't miss these Harlequin favorites by some of our most distinguished authors!

And now, you can receive a discount by ordering two or more titles!

HT#25409	THE NIGHT IN SHINING ARMOR by JoAnn Ross	$2.99	☐
HT#25471	LOVESTORM by JoAnn Ross	$2.99	☐
HP#11463	THE WEDDING by Emma Darcy	$2.89	☐
HP#11592	THE LAST GRAND PASSION by Emma Darcy	$2.99	☐
HR#03188	DOUBLY DELICIOUS by Emma Goldrick	$2.89	☐
HR#03248	SAFE IN MY HEART by Leigh Michaels	$2.89	☐
HS#70464	CHILDREN OF THE HEART by Sally Garrett	$3.25	☐
HS#70524	STRING OF MIRACLES by Sally Garrett	$3.39	☐
HS#70500	THE SILENCE OF MIDNIGHT by Karen Young	$3.39	☐
HI#22178	SCHOOL FOR SPIES by Vickie York	$2.79	☐
HI#22212	DANGEROUS VINTAGE by Laura Pender	$2.89	☐
HI#22219	TORCH JOB by Patricia Rosemoor	$2.89	☐
HAR#16459	MACKENZIE'S BABY by Anne McAllister	$3.39	☐
HAR#16466	A COWBOY FOR CHRISTMAS by Anne McAllister	$3.39	☐
HAR#16462	THE PIRATE AND HIS LADY by Margaret St. George	$3.39	☐
HAR#16477	THE LAST REAL MAN by Rebecca Flanders	$3.39	☐
HH#28704	A CORNER OF HEAVEN by Theresa Michaels	$3.99	☐
HH#28707	LIGHT ON THE MOUNTAIN by Maura Seger	$3.99	☐

Harlequin Promotional Titles

#83247	YESTERDAY COMES TOMORROW by Rebecca Flanders	$4.99	☐
#83257	MY VALENTINE 1993	$4.99	☐
	(short-story collection featuring Anne Stuart, Judith Arnold, Anne McAllister, Linda Randall Wisdom)		

(limited quantities available on certain titles)

	AMOUNT	$
DEDUCT:	10% DISCOUNT FOR 2+ BOOKS	$
ADD:	POSTAGE & HANDLING	$
	($1.00 for one book, 50¢ for each additional)	
	APPLICABLE TAXES*	$ _____
	TOTAL PAYABLE	$ _____
	(check or money order—please do not send cash)	

To order, complete this form and send it, along with a check or money order for the total above, payable to Harlequin Books, to: **In the U.S.:** 3010 Walden Avenue, P.O. Box 9047, Buffalo, NY 14269-9047; **In Canada:** P.O. Box 613, Fort Erie, Ontario, L2A 5X3.

Name: _____

Address: _____ City: _____

State/Prov.: _____ Zip/Postal Code: _____

*New York residents remit applicable sales taxes.
Canadian residents remit applicable GST and provincial taxes.

HBACK-JM

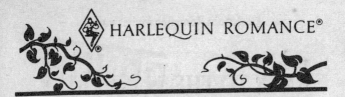

HARLEQUIN ROMANCE®

WELCOME BACK, MARGARET WAY!

After an absence of five years, Margaret Way—one of our most popular authors ever—returns to Romance!

Start the New Year with the excitement and passion of

ONE FATEFUL SUMMER
A brand-new Romance from Margaret Way

Available in January wherever Harlequin Books are sold.

HRMW

Harlequin Romance invites you...

BACK TO THE RANCH

As you enjoy your Harlequin Romance® BACK TO THE
RANCH stories each month, you can collect four proofs of
purchase to redeem for an attractive gold-toned charm bracelet
complete with five Western-themed charms. The bracelet will
make a unique addition to your jewelry collection or a
distinctive gift for that special someone.

One proof of purchase can be found in the back pages of each
BACK TO THE RANCH title...one every month until
May 1994.

To receive your gift, please fill out the information below and mail four (4) original proof-of-purchase coupons from any Harlequin Romance **BACK TO THE RANCH** title plus $2.50 for postage and handling (check or money order—do not send cash), payable to Harlequin Books, to: **IN THE U.S.**: P.O. Box 9056, Buffalo, NY, 14269-9056; **IN CANADA**: P.O. Box 621, Fort Erie, Ontario, L2A 5X3.

Requests must be received by June 30, 1994.

Please allow 4-6 weeks after receipt of order for delivery.

BACK TO THE RANCH

NAME: _____
ADDRESS: _____
_____
CITY: _____
STATE/PROVINCE: _____
ZIP/POSTAL CODE: _____
ACCOUNT NO.: _____

ONE PROOF OF PURCHASE   091 KAX